"I can't believe it's you," Kate said.

"Believe it," Justin answered. He took a step closer, so close that drops from his wet hair spilled onto her nightshirt, so close she could smell the fresh scent of his soap, so close that all she could see was the uncertainty in his eyes.

So close that when Justin reached for her and pulled her to his wet, hard chest and kissed her, it seemed like the only thing in the world he could have done.

It was the kiss Kate had remembered, the one that made her forget who she was. She knew Chelsea and Connor were watching, but it didn't matter. Nothing mattered except feeling that way again.

Look for new titles in the
Ocean City series
coming soon from HarperPaperbacks

Love Shack

Fireworks

Boardwalk

And don't miss

Freshman Dorm—the Hit Series!
by Linda A. Cooney

Now twenty-eight titles strong!

OCEAN CITY

Katherine Applegate

HarperPaperbacks
A Division of **HarperCollins***Publishers*

For Michael,
who did the heavy lifting

HarperPaperbacks *A Division of* HarperCollins*Publishers*
10 East 53rd Street, New York, N.Y. 10022

Copyright © 1993 by Daniel Weiss Associates, Inc.
and Katherine Applegate
Cover art copyright © 1993 Daniel Weiss Associates, Inc.

All rights reserved. No part of this book may be used or reproduced in any manner whatsoever without written permission of the publisher, except in the case of brief quotations embodied in critical articles and reviews. For information address Daniel Weiss Associates, Inc., 33 West 17th Street, New York, New York 10011.

Produced by Daniel Weiss Associates, Inc., 33 West 17th Street, New York, New York 10011.

First printing: July, 1993

Printed in the United States of America

HarperPaperbacks and colophon are trademarks of HarperCollins*Publishers*

10 9 8 7 6 5 4 3 2 1

ONE

"Are we there yet? This is getting very, very serious. I'm not kidding."

"Just hang on," Kate Quinn said. "I swear, Chels, you've got the bladder control of a two-year-old."

Chelsea Lennox shifted her position on the sizzling-hot front seat of Kate's battered red Buick convertible. "I *asked* you to pull over two Diet Pepsis and an iced tea ago."

"You can pee when we get there." Kate lowered her shades and smiled. "It'll be your first experience of Ocean City. A real Hallmark moment."

Kate was in no mood to stop now, not when they were almost to O.C. Not when she could already smell the salt and sweat and suntan lotion on the wind.

The scrub-pine forest that lined the highway suddenly gave way to sand and sea grass, and Kate drank in the air. Intoxicating. It was hers, all hers, all summer. And this time she'd be on her own. No more visits to a rented beach cottage with her family. No more curfews, no more rules.

And, she thought with sudden wistfulness, no more Justin.

Maybe it was the hot sun teasing her bare shoulders, maybe it was the promise of the ocean in the breeze, but the closer she got to Ocean City, the more she found herself recalling his kisses last summer. Not just any kisses, either. The slow-burn, take-your-time, lingering kind, the kind custom-made for a sultry afternoon at the beach. The kind of kisses that made you forget everything except you and him and maybe the sound of the waves breaking in the distance.

And now, heading back to Ocean City, they were all Kate could remember of the summer before. The kisses of a guy who was long gone by now, far away with his own memories of Ocean City.

"Can't you pick up the pace, Kate?"

Chelsea's pleading voice snapped Kate back to reality. "Two more miles," Kate assured her. "I promise."

"That's what you said two miles ago." Chelsea laced her hands behind her head and turned her face to the sun. "Next time I'm riding the 'hound. At least buses have bathrooms."

"They also have twitching, drooling old men who want to sleep in your lap," Kate added. Chelsea was your basic first-class-only kind of traveler. Her parents were quite well-off—not polo-playing, butler-hiring wealthy, but they were rich enough to keep their youngest daughter from ever riding in something as common as a bus. "When have you ever been on a Greyhound, anyway?"

"I've seen the commercials," Chelsea said, propping her legs up on the dashboard. "Besides, a girl can dream, can't she? From now on, I intend to live dangerously."

"Dangerous" was not the first word that came to mind when Kate thought of Chelsea. Unpredictable, impulsive, a little flaky sometimes, but Chels was too nice to be a danger to anyone.

Kate glanced across the seat. Chelsea had one arm draped outside the car, her hand open to catch the wind. With the toes of her left foot, she fiddled with the radio knob, searching for a better station. Her mahogany skin glistened with a fine sheen of sweat. She was wearing a purple bathing-suit top, yellow biker shorts, one red

3

plastic sandal, and big square earrings that combined all three colors in a swirling design. Chelsea had made them herself, a sort of retro tie-dye look for the ears. She'd made a smaller pair for Kate, too, in gentler tones of brown and gold to match Kate's wardrobe of hiking shorts and T-shirts.

That was the difference between them. If Kate was earth tones, Chelsea was all bright colors and swirling energy. She was a talented artist who saw the world not in simple blues and greens and reds, but in teals and emeralds and vermillions, a person of sudden decisions and instant enthusiasms. Chelsea was sweet and maybe a little sheltered, but she had a rebellious streak Kate loved. It kept her just unpredictable enough to make life interesting.

Kate had never really allowed herself to feel sheltered and safe. She'd always gone out of her way to look for challenges, from rock climbing and skydiving to chasing A's and academic honors.

She was tall, slender, and blond, although her hair was beginning to darken over time from its original spun gold. Her eyes were clear blue. She thought of them as cool and penetrating, while Chelsea's were laughing, coy, and inviting.

They laughed a lot together, always had, even

4

in tough times, and they'd been inseparable since they'd met in sixth grade. Kate had been running for class president, and Chelsea had volunteered to make her campaign posters. Somehow Chelsea had gotten hold of a giant roll of paper from the local newspaper and made a fifty-foot-long ad for Kate, featuring everything from wild campaign promises—*Ten Bucks for Every A!*—to wicked caricatures of the teachers. Kate had won in a landslide. She'd always credited Chelsea's artwork, but Chelsea maintained that Kate, everyone's confidant, everyone's trusted friend, would have won anyway.

"Close your eyes," Kate instructed as she rounded the familiar curve.

Across a broad, flat bay was a thin strip of land, covered from end to end with everything from high-rise condos to tiny wooden cottages. Ocean City. A last, fragile outpost of land in the huge expanse of shimmering ocean, it lay before them like a fragile sliver of moon in a vast blue-gray sky. It should have sunk long ago under the weight of all the hotels and restaurants and well-fed tourists. It was breathtaking and trashy, serene and wild. And it was theirs for an entire summer.

"Open," Kate said. "And behold Paradise."

Chelsea yanked off her sunglasses. "Whoa," she

murmured. "Would you look at that? 'Ocean City Best Body on the Beach Contest.'" She pointed to a billboard on the side of the road. Two freshly painted Ken and Barbie types waved at them seductively.

"That tacky sign is the first thing you notice about your new home?" Kate wailed.

"Can you blame me? Did you see the biceps on that poster boy?" Then she turned her gaze toward the town itself and let out a satisfyingly impressive gasp. "I didn't know Ocean City was so big."

"It isn't, really," Kate said. "It's long, but at its widest there are only about four blocks between the bay and the ocean. Of course, on a busy summer day they do manage to squeeze a hundred thousand people in there, give or take a few."

"It looks like Oz."

"It *is* Oz. Oz with beaches."

"Oz with guys." Chelsea grinned. "Shirtless, well-muscled guys."

"Oz with intelligent, sensitive men who'll love us for our minds, not just for our bodies."

"That's what I like about you, Kate," Chelsea joked. "You lead such a rich fantasy life."

She reached to crank up the old Beach Boys tune on the radio as they eased onto the two-mile-long causeway that spanned the bay. Windsurfers glided along on either side, and closer to the far shore two people were racing Jet Skis, painting curving white wakes on the placid surface of the bay.

"No!" Chelsea suddenly shouted. "The drawbridge is going up!"

Traffic slowed to a stop as the bridge rose toward vertical. "Relax. It won't take long." Kate pointed over the side of the bridge. "Look at the sailboat. It's so quaint."

"This is not quaint," Chelsea said through clenched teeth. "This is not even remotely quaint. This is now a matter of life and death and saving what's left of your upholstery." She pushed open the door and climbed out.

"Can't you hold it for a few more minutes?" Kate asked with a laugh, just as an extremely good-looking guy in a Jeep pulled to a stop beside them.

"No. I'm going to that Winnebago up there. They have mini-potties. Traveling cans. Whatever you call them."

"Portajohns," said the guy in the Jeep.

Kate glanced over just long enough to register a wide grin and a dimple.

She watched, grinning, as Chelsea hobbled off. The incredible thing was, Chelsea would probably talk the people in that house on wheels into letting her in. Then she'd talk them into making her a quick sandwich, too.

The Winnebago door opened and an elderly woman in a bright pink sundress leaned out. Chelsea spoke with her for a moment, then glanced back and gave Kate the thumbs-up.

"Here for the summer?"

Kate turned. The guy had moved over to the passenger's seat of his Jeep. He was very blond, very tan, very gorgeous. He had on a scuzzy blue YALE T-shirt and a pair of neon-yellow sunglasses. She wondered what color his eyes were and put her money on blue.

"Alec Daniels." He lowered the shades. Baby blues. Bingo.

"Kate." Her last name could wait. He could be an ax murderer, for all she knew.

"Looks like your friend made it just in time."

"We've been on the road all day," Kate explained. She wiped her damp forehead with the back of her arm. With the car standing still, the intense June sun was baking the ragged black seats. Even in her pale blue T-shirt and frayed cutoffs, she was overheating. She wished she'd thought to wear her new bathing suit for the trip.

"So you doing the summer thing in O.C., or just down here for the weekend?"

8

"I have a job. An internship, really, at a place called Safe Seas."

"Yeah, I've heard of it. The fish people."

"Marine conservation."

"Right. Fish, like I said. I'm guarding with the Beach Patrol."

Her heart picked up speed a little. Justin had been a lifeguard last summer. Alec might have known him, might even still be in touch with him. "Did you guard here last summer?"

"Nope. This is my first year."

Kate felt strangely disappointed, until she reminded herself she didn't care about Justin anymore. He could be lifeguarding in Maui and it wouldn't matter to her.

"I just graduated," Alec said. He shook his head, as if he couldn't quite believe it. "Free at last."

Kate flicked the gold tassel swinging from her rearview mirror. "Me too." She pointed toward the Winnebago. "Both of us, actually."

Up ahead the drawbridge finally began to lower. A few cars blared their horns, a mixture of impatience and celebration. Kate beeped hers, too, mostly to get Chelsea in gear.

"I don't suppose you know any place in town to stay, do you?" Alec asked.

"We're staying in a cottage the Safe Seas people lined up for me." Alec's eyes lit up. "But they tell me it's tiny," she added quickly. "Minuscule. Barely big enough for us. Incredibly—"

"Small," Alec finished for her. "No prob. I got a late start on house hunting. And I hear that O.C.'s a total madhouse. By March the whole place is booked. My family came here for years when I was a kid, and we always used to reserve a place a year in advance."

Traffic began to move forward. Kate leaned on her horn and was relieved to see the Winnebago door open. "Good luck," she yelled to Alec.

"You too," he said, putting his Jeep into gear.

Chelsea leaned out the door to the Winnebago, and Kate drove up to meet her. Chelsea hopped in on the left side, into the backseat, then bounced up into the front. As she settled into the seat, Alec honked and gave a good-bye wave.

"Jeez, Kate. I leave you for five minutes and you're already putting the moves on some guy," Chelsea teased. "You know, I have the feeling this summer's going to be good for both of us. I'm going to wipe the slate clean and start my life over. And in the meantime, I'll be here to make sure you *have* a life."

"Me? I happen to have the most incredible

summer job in the world waiting for me."

"I meant a *love* life."

"How about if I just fall in love with my work?"

"You can count only so many fish eggs."

"I *won't* be counting fish eggs, Chelsea," Kate replied. Or would she? She'd been so excited about being selected for an internship at the Safe Seas Foundation that she'd forgotten to ask for a job description.

Kate's gaze was drawn to the top of the Ocean City Grand Hotel, the tallest point on the skyline. It sat on one of the nicest stretches of beach—the beach where she'd first met Justin. The same beach, in fact, where they'd very nearly made love late one evening after the lights of the boardwalk were extinguished and the moon had sunk under the horizon.

That's all over, she reminded herself firmly. He'd moved away and she'd moved on. And today was a day for new beginnings.

They picked up steam and rolled over the top of the drawbridge, the sweet, salty wind whipping their hair to a frenzy. The city lay at their feet, the ocean beyond, beckoning like an old friend.

"We're here, Kate," Chelsea cried.

"We're free."

11

"And we're *dangerous*!"

They were finally on their own. Free from families, free from expectations, free, at last, from high school.

And maybe even free, Kate hoped, from memories.

TWO

Kate pulled the car to a rolling stop at the turnoff for Forty-third Street. Like most of the streets that ran east-west across Ocean City, it was only two blocks long, dead-ending against the board-walk, the wooden sidewalk that ran along the beach.

"You see any spaces down there?" Kate asked.

"Nope."

"Great. We're living on a street where there's no parking. Let's try the next block."

"Look at that," Chelsea said, pointing to the string of tiny, colorful shops lining the main drag. "Bikinis, soft-shell-crab sandwiches, boogie boards, bait, and triple-X videos, all in one convenient location. It's better than the mall back home."

They didn't find an open space until Forty-fifth Street. Kate turned off the car, and as the engine wheezed into silence, the familiar, soothing sound of crashing waves met her ears. A sea gull swooped close to check out the car for leftovers, then departed with a raucous cry.

"Hey, we're right at the beach, aren't we?" Chelsea asked excitedly as she searched through the backseat for her missing sandal.

"Everywhere in Ocean City is right at the beach," Kate pointed out. "That's why they named this place Ocean City, instead of Mountain City or Desert City." She fished a comb out of her purse and began the painful task of dragging it through her wind-snarled hair.

"Found it!" Chelsea waved her sandal in the air triumphantly.

"I don't suppose you found the rest of my Milky Way, did you?"

Chelsea made a face as she slipped on her sandal. "Put it this way. If you need another sugar fix, you'd better find yourself a straw."

Kate shrugged and stashed her comb in her bag. "Come on. The cottage can wait two more minutes. I want to check out the beach."

She shot out of the car and dashed toward the wooden steps that led to the boardwalk. They were sizzling against her bare feet, but she didn't care. The water would feel just that

14

much more heavenly when she dove in.

"Hey! Wait up," Chelsea cried. "It's not going anywhere." But nothing could stop Kate now, not when the ocean was this close. When she reached the boardwalk, the mingled smells of caramel corn and french fries greeted her. She dodged a skateboarder rocketing along obliviously. She barely avoided a second skateboarder, apologized as she bumped into a middle-aged couple in matching green outfits, and leaped onto the sand.

"It's incredible!" she heard Chelsea yell behind her. And it was. Kate flew across the beach, reveling in the resistance of the burning-hot sand. Even with her eyes trained on the water, she took in everything around her. The toddler sporting a drooping wet diaper and a pail of sand. The little boy collecting shells, zinc oxide striping his face like war paint. The high-school girl lying on her stomach, discreetly untying her bathing-suit top to avoid tan lines. The two old women playing cards beneath a bright yellow umbrella. The well-muscled guy in cutoffs, slathering coconut-scented oil on his giggling girlfriend.

And then, finally, Kate was there. At the water's edge she dropped her bag and plunged in.

The water was shockingly cold as she let herself fall into a gentle wave. She came up laughing, flinging her hair to throw off the water. The pockets of her shorts were half filled with sand. Her T-shirt clung to her chest.

This was wonderful. This was why she was here.

She rubbed her eyes and focused on the shore. Chelsea was there, shaking her head and grinning. "Hey, Gidget. I think you ran too far."

"I love the ocean," Kate cried, smoothing her hair back over her head. "Come on in. It's freezing."

"I think I'll pass. The landlady already knows *you're* coming. I'm the surprise. I don't know if soaking wet is my best first impression."

"Come on. Aren't you hot?"

"Don't tempt me, Kate. You know I have no self-control."

Kate struggled against the tug of the retreating wave as it sifted the sand beneath her feet, trying to draw her out to sea. Suddenly Chelsea threw down her bag and came splashing in with a joyous scream. She stumbled, reached out to Kate for support, and sent both of them face-first into a breaker.

"Nice move," Kate said, giving Chelsea a hand up.

"Great. Now I'm soaked," Chelsea lamented. "Fortunately, with spandex, who can tell? Plus"— she ran a hand through her hair—"my hair is waterproof, losing none of its bounce or luster."

Kate smiled in response, but her eyes were drawn to the lifeguard stand about fifty yards away. The guard was standing in his chair, blowing his whistle at a kid in the water. From this distance . . . but no. The hair was wrong. The shoulders too narrow. It wasn't Justin.

Kate turned her attention back to Chelsea. "I'm glad you decided to come, Chels," she said.

"Even though I waited till the last possible minute to decide?"

"Yeah."

"Even though I slowed you down by a day?"

"And even though you ragged on my driving for three hundred and twenty-five miles," Kate assured her. "You're not having any second thoughts, are you?"

"Me?" She looked around, taking it all in. "No way. O.C. is absolutely, perfectly, metaphysically correct."

Kate smiled. It was Chelsea's favorite phrase.

"Besides," Chelsea added, "have I ever had second thoughts about anything?"

"No, unfortunately. Still, I wouldn't blame you. It *was* kind of a whim, coming along with me. You were going to kick back and relax all summer with Greg."

"Greg? Hmm, the name rings a bell . . ."

Chelsea said as they waded back to shore and grabbed their bags. Warm, dry sand stuck between their toes and dusted their legs as they walked.

"You remember Greg—your boyfriend for most of senior year? Tall, good-looking guy, with an ego the size of his wallet?"

"Oh, *that* Greg." Chelsea shrugged. "You know what they say"—she grinned—"out of sight, out of mind."

They recrossed the wide, hot beach, pausing at the edge of the boardwalk to brush off the sand. Again Kate ran a comb through her hair, wringing out the saltwater.

"Which way to our happy new home?" Chelsea asked.

"Thataway," Kate said excitedly, pointing down the boardwalk. "I hope it comes with towels."

Chelsea stood waiting on the sidewalk while Kate went to talk to the landlady. Kate was supposed to be the only tenant, and there was no point in seeming pushy. True, they *were* being pushy, bringing Chelsea in at the last minute like this. But there was no point in *seeming* that way.

She leaned against the hood of a car, trying to look casual, while straining to hear the muffled conversation between Kate and the dainty elderly woman.

Sand crunched in Chelsea's sandals, and when she looked down she saw that water, dripping slowly from her hair and clothes, had made a pretty abstract pattern of dark spots on the sidewalk. It wasn't a bad start to a painting, actually.

This place had plenty of potential, artistically speaking. Not that Chelsea was the kind of artist who'd do those sea-gulls-on-the-beach oils that sold like crazy at mall art shows. No. Sea gulls were not her idea of subject matter. She did big, abstract paintings, brimming with color and light. Paintings, her parents never failed to remind her, that would never provide the basis for a reliable income, or keep her in the style to which she was accustomed. No, law school would provide a reliable income. And a slow, lingering death by boredom.

Kate was coming back down the walkway, striding purposefully. Chelsea smiled. Kate always strode purposefully, which was no fun when they were mall-crawling. She shopped like a guided missile.

"All set?" Chelsea asked hopefully.

"Oh, yes. All set. For someone else."

"What are you talking about?" Chelsea took

Kate's arm. She'd seen the look before. It was Kate's coping-with-disaster look. "Wouldn't she go for the extra roommate?"

Kate stared straight ahead, taking deep, even breaths.

"Whoa," Chelsea said, observing Kate's yoga breaths. "This *is* serious. Maybe if I go talk to her, show her what a fine, upstanding specimen of today's youth I am, she might let me stay."

Kate executed an annoyingly slow *out* breath. "Go for it," she said. "I hope you like your new roommate."

"What *are* you talking about?"

"She rented the cottage to someone else."

"What? But it was all arranged!"

"When I didn't show up yesterday and this other girl came to the door, cash in hand, the landlady didn't feel like she had a choice. She called Safe Seas, but all she got was an answering machine." Kate began shaking her head slowly back and forth. "I should have called her," she muttered. "I should have called her. I *knew* I should have called her. Why didn't I call her?"

"Because you were too busy helping me pack all day," Chelsea answered. "And then you had to do the Last Supper thing with your family, and by the time you got home, you were afraid it was too late to call." Chelsea had an unsettling feeling deep inside, and it wasn't from the Milky Way she'd eaten en route. It was guilt. Her least-favorite emotion. "It's my fault, Kate. You know it is."

"No it isn't."

"Yes it is. C'mon, say it. It's my fault."

Another yoga breath, this time an *in*.

"Come on," Chelsea said gently. "Say it, Kate." She touched her friend's shoulder. "It'll make you feel better. Go ahead and—"

"It's your fault!" Kate threw back her head. "It's your fault I had to sit around for an extra day while you made up your mind and now we're homeless in a city that's been booked up since last year and I'm probably going to lose my internship because I don't even have an address and I'll have to get a job making caramel corn on the boardwalk!"

"I'm sorry." Chelsea looked at the landlady's house and at the small gray cottage beside it. Their home. Her and Kate's. "If I'd had my act together, we'd already be relaxing on the porch of our new house by now."

Kate stared blankly at the cottage. "There *is* no porch," she muttered.

Good. She was taking the bait. "No yard, either," Chelsea said casually. "No view. No nothing, really."

"Don't try to manipulate me. You don't get it,

21

Chelsea. This town is already booked solid. Everything's rented." She sighed. "We're doomed."

"Okay. If you say so, we're doomed. But maybe this was all meant to be."

"Chelsea, we're homeless. Do you realize that? We've been on our own"—Kate consulted her watch—"exactly seven hours and twenty-two minutes, and our lives are already falling apart."

"We could stay in a hotel for a few days."

"A few days? At a hundred bucks a day? We can't afford to use our rent money on a hotel." Kate closed her eyes. "If we don't find something quick, we're in deep trouble. We may have to go and live in the woods, scratching out a bare existence, living on bark and roots, using leaves for toilet paper."

Chelsea rolled her eyes. Obviously Kate was recovering. "You'd love living in the woods," she pointed out. "All that fresh air."

"Better than crawling home in defeat," Kate replied darkly.

"No way. We can't go home. Greg and my parents would say 'I told you so.' You know they didn't think I could handle being on my own." Chelsea crossed her arms over her chest. "And anyway, I like the *feel* of this town, Kate. I just have this sense that everything will work out. I don't know how, and I don't know where, but we're staying here in Ocean City."

THREE

Grace Caywood lifted the glass from her tray, snagged a small paper cocktail napkin with her little finger, and deposited the drink on the starched white tablecloth. The middle-aged man looked up and smiled. His eyes drifted down the length of her body. A quick look, but not so quick that his wife didn't notice it.

Great. There goes the tip from this table, Grace thought. "I'll give you folks a while to look over the menu and enjoy your drinks; then I'll be back to take your order," she said smoothly. She'd been working at The Claw only since graduation a couple weeks earlier, but already Grace had said the same line about a million times.

At least she wasn't working at some dive on the boardwalk. The Claw was a fairly pricey restaurant: white linen tablecloths, rosebuds on the tables. Many more tourists ate there than locals. It was a two-story affair, with a club featuring live music on the bottom and the restaurant on the upper level, where the diners had a panoramic view of the beach. So far the tips had been pretty good, and Grace liked her fellow waiters, most of whom were college students working in O.C. for the summer.

She was heading back toward the kitchen when one of them fell into step beside her. "Waiter meeting," he said in a low, conspiratorial voice.

Grace shot him a grateful look. "I'll be right there. I just have to drop a ticket in the kitchen."

She approached the swinging kitchen door and kicked it open. It was hard on her feet, not to mention her shoes, but she'd picked up the move from watching the other, more experienced waiters.

Grace pulled a ticket from her apron pocket, slammed it on the stainless-steel counter, and yelled, "Ordering!"

The young head cook cocked an eyebrow at her. "You can order me to do anything," he said.

"Okay. How about grilling yourself to a nice medium rare?"

The cook grinned and pretended to shiver. "I love it when you talk tough."

But Grace was already on her way out of the kitchen, ducking to avoid a fellow waiter carrying a heavily loaded tray. "Hey, waiter meeting," she whispered.

"Gotta pass on that," he answered. "I have a big table that's running my butt off."

Grace beelined for the bar, where three other waiters—two college-aged guys and a woman in her twenties—were waiting impatiently. Anton, the bartender, was shaking a chrome mixing cup.

"Lay 'em out," Anton said.

Grace obeyed, lifting five small glasses from beneath the counter and setting them upright in a row on the bar.

"Are we sure that Frank is in his office?" one of the waiters asked nervously.

Mike, who was the headwaiter at The Claw, shrugged. "Would I call a waiter meeting if our esteemed manager was out and about? He's in his office having a 'discussion' with Jennifer. A *long* discussion with Jennifer, if you know what I mean."

Grace knew exactly. Frank's "secret" romance with Jennifer, one of the cocktail waitresses who worked in the club, was common knowledge at The Claw.

Anton finished shaking his mixing cup and began pouring quickly into each of the five glasses. "What are these?" Grace asked, eyeing the greenish color suspiciously.

"Melon-ball shooters," Anton said.

"Waiter meeting in session," Mike announced.

All five raised their glasses and drank them down in a single gulp. Grace felt the familiar warm glow as the alcohol reached her stomach.

"Back to it," Mike said. He took off with the others. "Got any extra?" Grace asked Anton.

Anton hesitated, then poured the last ounce from the mixing cup into Grace's glass. "Rough night?" he asked.

Grace drank the sweet liquid. "Aren't they all?" She liked Anton. Possibly because he was one of the few guys in the place who wasn't at all interested in her for her looks. In fact, Anton was much more interested in Mike.

"Getting fed up already, Grace? Hell, you've only been working here a couple weeks."

"It's not work, Anton," she said. Grace took in a deep breath. The air smelled of spilled beer and drifting cigarette smoke. "I'm moving out of my mother's house tomorrow."

"Going it alone, huh? Things that bad?" he asked.

"Bad enough that I need to be on my own," Grace confessed. "I'm making money now, and everyone says as we get further into the busy part of the season, the tips will keep getting better."

"True enough. And if it's bad at home—well, hey, I say bail."

"Easy to say," Grace pointed out. "Hard to actually do. I've got a brother, Bo, who's fifteen. . . ." She drifted off. She didn't want to think about it too much. The guilt would hurt, and the hurt would just make her long for another drink.

Grace gazed off across the dining room. Huge floor-to-ceiling windows opened onto the boardwalk. The sea beyond was beginning to grow gray and misty as the sun's rays weakened. In the distance she could just make out a lifeguard running down the beach. She wondered if it was Justin Garrett. She hadn't seen him in those cute red lifeguard trunks since last summer. As a matter of fact, she hadn't seen much of him at all, not lately. She'd have to look him up one of these days. For old times' sake.

"Excuse me, sir?" A pretty black girl about Grace's age was leaning over the bar.

"Yes?" Anton asked, wiping his hands with a bar towel.

"Can I get some quarters?" She gave him a hopeful look. "My friend and I have tons of phone calls to make."

"How many?"

"I guess about ten dollars' worth, if you can spare them."

"No problem." Anton pulled a roll of quarters from the cash drawer and exchanged them for two five-dollar bills.

The girl thanked him, flashed a killer smile, and headed back toward the hostess stand at the entrance, where a tall blond girl stood waiting, her head buried in a newspaper. She had a pen in her mouth and a look of deep concentration on her face.

"Bet they're looking for a place," Anton said.

"Aren't we all?" Grace muttered as she craned her neck to check on her tables.

"Hey, if you need a place to crash for a few days—"

"Thanks, Anton," Grace said. "But I'm sure I'll find something."

"Too bad you're getting such a late start. Most of the good rentals will be taken."

Grace sighed. "As long as I'm not at home, anything will be an improvement."

"We're wasting our time," Kate said for the third time in an hour. "We can ride up and down every street in this town and we'll never see a for-rent sign."

It would be dark soon. The sun was already

low over the bay, and at the south end of town, the neon lights of the Ferris wheel and tilt-a-whirl were flickering to life. The cool, damp air made her long for the windbreaker she'd packed away at the bottom of her suitcase.

"What's the worst that can happen?" Chelsea asked. "Maybe we'll find a motel room."

"We can't afford a motel room. If we don't find a house, we're going into the woods and live with the wolves."

"There are no wolves around here," Chelsea muttered. "Look. That motel sign says it has bargain rates. I'll bet we could afford it. We've got— how much was it again?"

"One thousand, four hundred and nine dollars," Kate said patiently. Money management was not Chelsea's strong point.

"We are *loaded,* aren't we?"

"We are also homeless. And don't forget we need to make this last. This is all our worldly savings, plus our graduation money." She threw up her hands, then quickly grabbed the wheel again. "It shows you how bogus most of what we learned in high school was. I mean, did we ever have a class in what to do when you're wandering around homeless?"

Chelsea threw a folded-up newspaper into the backseat and groaned. "We've read every ad.

We've been to every bulletin board in town. I spent eight dollars and seventy-five cents on phone calls in that restaurant. I'm ready to admit it now. We are officially desperate."

"Don't panic," Kate said. "I'll think of something."

"I still have one more plan."

"Yes, I know. And I get the backseat."

They paused at a light. "Hey, check out the water slide across the street," Chelsea said. "And they have Putt-Putt golf, too!" She leaned her head on the dashboard and moaned. "I can't leave town yet. Do you realize I've never actually Putt-Putted?"

"Put that on your list, right behind the Greyhound toilet."

The light changed, and a pickup truck filled to capacity with guys roared past them in the right lane. They whooped and waved, and one of them shouted out the address for a "major party tonight."

"A lot of June bugs out on the road already," Kate remarked.

Chelsea sat up. "What bugs?"

"That's what the locals call the high-school and college kids who show up here the start of summer."

They drove on for a few minutes in silence.

30

"Maybe we can find something tomorrow," Chelsea said. "You could call the people at the Foundation—" Suddenly she stopped in mid-sentence. "Turn around!" she screamed.

Kate screeched to a halt. "What is it? Did I hit something? A squirrel? A tourist?"

"Turn around now and burn rubber," Chelsea ordered. "I just saw my dream house."

A woman in a station wagon gave Kate the finger as she attempted to pull a U-turn across four lanes of traffic. Kate waved back pleasantly. "Chelsea, I doubt—"

"It looked perfect, Kate. This huge white Victorian house right down by the bay, and—get this—there was some old guy putting out a for-rent sign."

Kate pulled up alongside the house. Sure enough, there in the middle of the yard was a gray-haired man pounding a sign into the lawn.

"It's beautiful," Kate said. The house might have been a little run-down, but still, it oozed charm from every shingle.

"And it's on the bay! And it has a porch!" Chelsea reached for the door handle. "Let's go talk to him. If he asks if I have a job, tell him—I don't know—tell him I'm with the government."

"I'm afraid it's going to be way too expensive, Chels," Kate said. "It's huge."

"It won't hurt to ask." Chelsea was out of the car before Kate could object.

"Help you girls?" said the old man as he gave the sign one last pound.

"Great house," Chelsea said.

"Yep. You lookin' for a place, by chance?" the man asked, eyeing them speculatively.

"How much is the rent?" Kate asked, climbing out to join Chelsea.

"Thirteen hundred and seventy-five."

"A season?" Chelsea asked hopefully.

The man laughed. "Twenty years ago, maybe. Nope, that's per month, young lady. Course, with five bedrooms, that's just two seventy-five a month split five ways. I had it rented, but these damn college kids changed their minds at the last minute."

"Imagine that," Kate said. "Kids today. Well, we'd better be going." Kate gave her friend a we're-outta-here nod, but Chelsea ignored her.

"I don't suppose we could just take a little peek inside?" Chelsea asked.

"Sure. Sun's nearly down, so you're not going to get as good a view of the bay as you might, though. Name's Joe Mabrey, by the way," the old man said as he held open the door for Chelsea.

"I'm Chelsea Lennox. And that's Kate Quinn.

The rest of our roommates won't be here for a few more days."

Kate lagged behind while Chelsea and the old man headed inside. There was no point in following them. Why bother? Why tempt herself with what she couldn't have?

A moment later Chelsea stuck her head out the door. "Kate! It's got a stone fireplace!"

On the other hand, what could it hurt to look?

Inside it was even better than she'd imagined. Incredibly high ceilings. Polished wood floors that shone like still ponds. An actual crystal chandelier in the dining room. Claw-foot tubs in two of the bathrooms. A kitchen with two refrigerators. Sure, there were some signs of wear and tear—wallpaper peeling back to reveal earlier patterns, furniture with stains she'd rather not speculate about, and a stove that predated the Flintstones. But still. It *was* an incredible house.

While Joe and Chelsea chatted in the living room, Kate wandered onto the porch to check out the view. At the end of a long, sloping yard was a large boathouse and a pier. The bay was in a gentle mood this evening, and the last red rays of the sun skipped off the waves like stones.

She stood there, lost in the tranquil beauty. Someday she'd live in a place just like this.

Chelsea joined her on the porch. "Where's Joe?" Kate asked.

"He went home."

"Home? You mean he just *left* us here in his house?"

"*Our* house," Chelsea corrected her after a long pause.

Kate stood perfectly still. "For a minute there, I thought you said *our* house."

Chelsea grinned. Then she pressed something small and cold into Kate's hand.

"What's this?" Kate asked.

"Your key. Welcome home."

FOUR

"Chels," Kate said slowly, "tell me the truth. You didn't give that man all our money, did you? Because that would have been really, really . . . not all that smart. And I know you would never do anything that really, really not all that smart without asking me first."

"I couldn't ask you," Chelsea argued. "You don't always do what you know you want to do."

"That's because I'm what's known as *sane*."

"You know, they say life is what happens while you're making other plans," Chelsea recited.

"You know what else they say? *You can't always get what you want.*"

"Look, we'll get roommates," Chelsea interrupted. "There are plenty of desperate people just like us out there looking for a place to stay."

Chelsea leaned against the porch railing.

"I don't want to live with desperate people," Kate said. "I don't like desperate people."

"I *had* to grab it, Kate," Chelsea insisted. "What other choice did we have? You didn't want to go home, did you?"

"You took the money out of my purse just like that?"

"It was half my money. And anyway, you left it in the car. Which was pretty stupid, incidentally."

"We'll just go see Joe in the morning," Kate said quietly, more to herself than to Chelsea. "We'll explain that you forgot to take your medication today, and I'm sure he'll give us the money back."

"Hey, look on the bright side. We don't have to live in the woods. Or run back to our parents."

"No danger of that," Kate pointed out. "We have exactly thirty-four dollars left, Chelsea. That won't even buy us enough gas to get halfway home." She slumped onto a rusty wrought-iron bench. "I had this so carefully planned. It was all going to be so perfect, and look—nothing is going right. Nothing. I'm finally on my own, and my life is falling apart." Kate paused, catching her breath.

She gave Chelsea an apologetic shrug. "Sorry,

Chels. It's just that right before I left this morning, my dad told me how sure he was that I would handle being on my own perfectly."

"Really? My dad gave me ten-to-one odds I'd be home by July."

Kate swallowed past the hard lump in her throat. "They expect so much of me, Chels. My dad went on and on about how hard it was for him and my mom to let me go. How hard it was for them not to worry about me every second, ever since—"

Ever since they'd watched Juliana, beautiful, sweet, funny Juliana, lowered into the ground four years ago. Kate couldn't bring herself to say her sister's name out loud.

Chelsea reached over and patted Kate's shoulder. "It'll be okay, Kate. I promise you won't disappoint them," she said gently. Kate started to respond, but just then something—or rather, someone—caught her eye. In the low rays of sunset he was only a dark silhouette on the pier, but there was no doubt he was a *he.* He stared out at the water, hands on hips, tall, broad-shouldered—a dark cutout against the molten sky. A dog sat patiently at his feet.

For the hundredth time that day, she thought of Justin, and for the hundredth time that day, she regretted it. She had more important things to worry about right now. Like survival.

Chelsea followed her gaze. "I'll bet that's the boathouse guy. There's a loft in the boathouse, and he rents it from Joe."

"Someone else already *lives* here?"

"Yeah, some guy."

"You moved us in with a perfect stranger? A *male* perfect stranger?"

"We'll hardly ever see him," Chelsea argued as she sat down next to Kate. "He has kitchen and bathroom privileges, but Joe said he pretty much keeps to himself."

"You're telling me he's allowed in the house? You're telling me I'm living with a guy I don't know?"

"Yes, but he's not a roommate, exactly. And speaking of roommates, here's the plan." Chelsea draped her arm around Kate's shoulders. "We'll run around tonight and put up some house-mates-needed signs on bulletin boards. If things don't work out, we can always back out, like those college kids did."

"And let Joe keep our thirteen hundred and seventy-five dollars?"

"You mean he gets to keep it either way?"

"That's why it's called a deposit, Chels. Didn't you pay any attention to that practical-economics class?"

"I knew I should have read the lease before I signed it. Oh well. I'm an artist. I can't be bothered with petty details."

"Welcome to the real world."

Chelsea swept her arm toward the glimmering bay. "Yeah," she whispered. "Isn't it great?"

For a few minutes they sat in silence. The distant drone of a motorboat floated across the bay, mingling with the chatter of the evening's first crickets. Next door, two little girls carrying glass jars played tag with the fireflies. Slowly the sun dissolved into the bay, and in the lingering twilight the stranger on the pier disappeared in shadow.

At last Chelsea spoke. "You're not going to smother me in the middle of the night while I sleep, are you?"

Kate laughed softly. "You know what this reminds me of?" she asked. "That time when we were in seventh grade and you signed me up for the boys' soccer-team tryouts without telling me."

"And you ended up being the best goalie they ever had."

"And the first ever to wear a training bra."

"That we know of, anyway." Chelsea grinned. "But I was right, wasn't I?"

"Yeah." Kate leaned her head on Chelsea's shoulder and sighed. "You were right."

"Trust me," Chelsea said, "I'm right about this, too. It was meant to be."

Kate awoke to find her pillow wet. It was not a surprise. It had happened many times before, whenever she dreamed about Juliana.

She wiped away the tears that still spilled from her eyes and rolled over onto her side. One of the springs in the couch cushions stabbed her. She and Chelsea had decided to camp out in the living room. They'd both admitted to feeling a little nervous in the big house, with its unfamiliar noises and dark shadows.

Chelsea was asleep, breathing easily on the other couch. Kate fumbled for her watch. The faint luminous dial showed three ten. In the kitchen the two refrigerators hummed a loud duet. A full moon streamed through the stained-glass window over the front door, sending ruby-colored light across the hardwood floor.

Kate knew she should roll over and go back to sleep, but she also knew it was impossible. She felt restless and jumpy and unsettled.

She slid out of her sleeping bag. The floor was cold on her bare feet, and the chilly air raised bumps on her arms. There was no need to worry about waking Chelsea—she'd spent enough nights sleeping over to know that nothing short of an earthquake would wake her. Still, Kate moved quietly, unwilling to disturb the perfect smooth surface of the night's silence.

She went to the door, opened it, and stepped onto the porch. It felt strange and exciting, being out all alone in a place she barely knew, dressed only in a thin nightshirt. The moon was low, plunging toward the western horizon, but still able to illuminate the few clouds, silver fleece against a sparkling black backdrop.

The cool breeze freshened her, swirling through her nightshirt, lifting tendrils of her hair. She walked down the stairs and onto the cold, dewy grass. It rustled softly as she moved, barely audible above the steady, throaty croak of a nearby frog.

She should have known she'd dream of Juliana. Changes in Kate's life always brought on memories of her older sister. Memories of Juliana lying impossibly still, her arm extended over the edge of her bed, stretched toward the nightstand as if she were pointing. Pointing at the brown bottle in which only a few of the tiny blue pills remained.

Kate reached the end of the pier. She didn't want to risk waking the person who rented the boathouse, but the water was drawing her closer, its voice a soft lapping sound that mingled with the creak of the pilings and the doleful call of a foghorn.

She walked softly, careful of the rough, splintered boards, but scarcely able to control the bundled, anxious energy in her limbs. At the end of the pier she knelt down. The water was at high tide, just inches below her. She dipped a hand in and was surprised by the warmth.

Kate turned to look up toward the house, ghostly white with dark, empty eyes for windows. Her home now, at least for a while. Her bathing suit was up there, neatly packed in a suitcase.

She glanced around at the dark boathouse. In one fluid movement she slipped off her nightshirt. For a brief, delicious moment, she stood there, letting the chill air caress her. Then she knelt again, swung her long legs over the side, and slipped into the water.

Kate had expected to touch a muddy bottom, but the water was too deep for that. It closed over her head, surprising her with its salty taste.

She surfaced and began breaststroking away from the pier. It was stupid, swimming alone in unfamiliar water at night. Stupid and thrilling and calming all at once.

As soon as she was away from the boathouse, she began swimming in earnest, stretching her arms out, cupping each handful of water, kicking powerfully, losing herself in the sheer physical exertion. She swam until her arms grew weak, her legs felt thick and heavy, her lungs burned. Then she rolled onto her back, reveling in the release of pent-up energy.

Maybe that had been Juliana's problem. Maybe she hadn't known how to burn away all the feelings of worry and guilt and self-doubt. Maybe that was all it was. Maybe.

Kate looked back toward shore, momentarily frightened at the undifferentiated, formless darkness, unable to see her objective. Then she saw a flash of light. A door opened in the boathouse. A low, dark shape came bounding out and ran up onto the lawn. Behind it came a slower form, a man.

Kate hoped he wouldn't see her nightshirt lying on the end of the dock. But all the dark figure seemed to be concerned with was getting his dog to do his business. After less than a minute, the dog came running back, following the man inside the boathouse.

Kate sighed in relief. Now she had a clear objective. The location of the boathouse was fixed in her mind. She closed her eyes and swam toward that goal.

*　　　*　　　*

Chelsea awoke to a numb left arm and the sound of slurping. She opened her eyes and saw the ceiling overhead—white-painted pressed tin in an ornate floral pattern. Bright summer sunshine danced along the edges. She blinked in confusion. This wasn't *her* ceiling, was it?

Then it hit her. She was in the new house. The great old house on the bay that she and Kate couldn't possibly afford.

She rolled over onto her back, her damp sleeping bag sticking to her. Man, it was hot. She wondered if this place had air conditioning.

She took a deep breath. There was something different about the air here. It was spicy, alive, full of possibilities, like breathing pure oxygen.

Chelsea grinned, closed her eyes, and opened them again. No, she was definitely not dreaming. Her parents were hundreds of miles away. Her boyfriend was hundreds of miles away. Her *life* was hundreds of miles away. She was here, they were there, and for once she could do exactly as she pleased.

Again she heard a slurping sound. Chelsea eased up onto her elbows to see where it was coming from.

"Good morning. Would you like a cup?"

"AHH!" Chelsea sat up straight and unconsciously gathered her sleeping bag around her.

A guy with long reddish-brown hair sat comfortably in the big, lumpy La-Z-Boy, sipping from a black mug. A tea-bag tag was draped over the side.

Chelsea's cry woke Kate, who seemed to awaken perfectly alert and functional. Her gaze went straight to their uninvited guest. "Who *are* you?" she demanded sternly.

"The name's Connor Riordan."

Chelsea noticed a very definite accent. Irish or Scottish—she wasn't awake enough to know which.

"What exactly are you doing here?" Kate rolled her legs off the other couch and began to extricate herself from her sleeping bag. *Easy enough for her,* Chelsea thought ruefully. *She's wearing a nightshirt.*

"I'm here about your notice." The word came out "nootice." Connor fumbled in his shirt pocket for a moment and pulled out a tiny slip of yellow paper torn from one of the ads they'd posted last night. "See?" He held it up as evidence. "All very innocent and aboveboard." He grinned, something he did with only one side of his mouth, as if he didn't want to commit himself to it.

Chelsea reached for her watch, which she'd stashed in the bottom of her shoe. "It's eight ten!" she complained.

"So it is." Connor nodded in agreement. "That's why I didn't wake you."

"But you made yourself at home in our kitchen?" Kate asked, her voice sliding up an octave.

Connor looked hurt. "It's my own tea, I assure you. I only used your water. I didn't think you'd begrudge a man a bit of water to make his simple cup of tea."

Chelsea couldn't help smiling. Connor's pained expression was such an obvious put-on.

"How did you get in?" Kate asked. "I distinctly remember locking the doors last night. I checked twice."

"And good for you, too," Connor said. "You can't be too careful. You never know who might come wandering into your home."

"That's *not* an answer." Kate stalked over and stood in front of him, arms crossed. Kate was good at being forceful when she had to be.

Connor climbed out of the chair, and Chelsea gave him a quick once-over. Suede jacket, well-worn jeans and boots. Square face and strong jaw, softened only by the long hair. She had the feeling that his smirk was very nearly permanent.

"The side door was open. The one in the kitchen," Connor said. "The other fellow left it unlocked."

"What *other* fellow?" Chelsea demanded.

"The fellow in the bathroom." Connor pointed with his free hand down the hall.

Chelsea craned her neck. The bathroom door was definitely closed, and light shone beneath it.

For a moment both girls stared in stunned silence at the door.

"Well, I can't go see who's in there," Chelsea said at last. "I'm not exactly dressed for entertaining gentlemen callers."

"What am I, dressed for success? I'm just wearing a shirt," Kate said.

"Yes, but *I'm* not," Chelsea said pointedly.

Kate nodded. "Yeah, that does kind of leave it up to me." She crept to the bathroom door and pressed her ear against the wood, listening intently. "I think someone's taking a shower in there," she reported.

"It's got to be the guy from the boathouse." Chelsea began to hop her way toward Kate, clutching the sleeping bag around her.

"I could turn my back while you dress," Connor offered.

"You *could* leave," Kate pointed out from the hallway.

"No need for that," Connor said blithely. He turned his back, made a point of staring at the

47

wall, and took a sip of his tea.

Quickly Chelsea slid out of her sleeping bag and yanked on her jeans. Just as she pulled the zipper up, Connor turned back around.

"Sorry," he said softly. "Thought you were finished." There was a trace of a smile on his lips as he turned back around.

Chelsea made a frantic grab for her shirt, slipping it on over her head. It was hard to know what to say. Maybe it *had* been an innocent mistake. On the other hand, Chelsea very much doubted that anything about Connor Riordan was innocent.

"It's okay now," Chelsea muttered.

Connor turned and met her eyes. "It was okay a moment ago too," he said.

"Someone's definitely taking a shower in there," Kate said.

Chelsea could clearly hear the sound of water. "He doesn't sing in the shower. I don't know if that's a good sign or a bad one."

"He should have asked us before he just came sneaking in."

"So right!" Connor said suddenly. "The fiend! Coming into the home of two defenseless young women. I won't have my new housemates treated with such callous disdain."

He strode into the hall and pounded on the

48

bathroom door. "Hey, you in there. Are you taking a shower?"

There was a pause. Then a muffled voice said, "Yeah. I'll be out in a minute."

"Ask him if he's the guy from the boathouse," Chelsea suggested.

"Are you the fellow from the boathouse?" Connor yelled.

"Yeah. Who the hell are you?"

"I'm the fellow from Ireland."

This time there was no response. After a moment the water stopped. They could make out the sound of a shower curtain being drawn open.

Chelsea and Kate jumped back as the door flew open.

A cloud of steam escaped, swirling around a guy barely covered by the towel wrapped around his waist. Water dripped off his dark hair onto the floor. Chelsea guessed from the rough stubble of beard that he hadn't gotten around to shaving this morning.

He glanced sourly at Kate and Chelsea, then turned on Connor. "Is there some reason why you're—"

Suddenly the annoyance in his eyes vanished. His face went completely blank. He turned back to Kate and stared hard.

"Justin?" Kate cried.

49

FIVE

"Justin?" This time Kate whispered it.

"Justin?" Chelsea echoed. *"Justin?"*

Connor extended his hand. "You must be Justin."

Justin ignored him. His eyes were locked on Kate. She wasn't sure what she saw in them. Shock? Hurt? Anger? For a long, tense moment, no one spoke.

"I can't believe it's you," she said to fill the silence, and to silence the sob in her throat.

"Believe it," he said. He took a step closer, so close that drops from his hair spilled onto her nightshirt, so close she could smell the fresh scent of his soap, so close that all she could see was the uncertainty in his eyes.

So close that when he reached for her and pulled her to his wet, hard chest and kissed her,

50

it seemed like the only thing in the world he could have done.

It was the kiss she'd remembered, the one that made her forget who she was. She knew Chelsea and Connor were watching, but it didn't matter. Nothing mattered except feeling that way again.

But there was something different in the way Justin touched her, an urgency that she hadn't remembered. His hands on her shoulders were gripping too tightly, his kiss was too searching. It wasn't right. It wasn't the same. She started to pull away and he let her go instantly.

"Whoa," Chelsea murmured, "talk about your welcome wagon."

For a moment, Justin stared at Kate, his mouth set in a determined line. He shook his head grimly. Then slowly he backed into the bathroom and closed the door.

Kate opened her mouth to cry, but no sound came out. She felt something squeeze her arm and realized it was Chelsea. "You better sit down before you fall down. You look like you're going into shock."

Kate stared at the bathroom door. When she didn't budge, Chelsea pulled her toward the living room.

"I should have known this would happen,"

Kate muttered. "I should have known, I should have known, I should have known."

"So it's fair to say you two have met before?" Connor asked.

The bathroom door opened again. Justin had shed his towel and put on red swim trunks and a tank top. His face was set in an emotionless scowl, and he brushed past them without a word. Seconds later the front door slammed.

"A man of few words," Connor said.

"Speaking of few words, spill it, Kate," Chelsea commanded. "What's this all about?"

Kate shook her head. "I can't stay here," she said. "Don't even argue with me, Chelsea, because there's no way I can stay in this house."

Half an hour later Justin settled back in his chair and let his eyes close to slits. He could still see that way, and it cut down on the harsh glare that penetrated even the dark sunglasses he wore while on the job.

He made a quick check of the beach. Far south, well out of his zone, there was a volleyball game going on. At the northern edge of his sight he could just make out the wooden platform they were building for the Best Body on the Beach contest.

Justin's chair sat about five feet off the

ground, enough to let him see over the tops of the small gray-green waves. Out beyond the surf line, he spotted a kid who looked to be about ten, clutching a foam boogie board and paddling awkwardly. Better keep an eye on that one. He had a feeling concentrating on his work today was going to be tough.

Kate. The name popped into his head again, for the hundredth, the thousandth time in the short while since he'd left the house. Kate.

He'd acted like a jerk, taking off without so much as a word to her. But what could he have said? She'd caught him off guard. It was unreal that she would show up right outside his bathroom door. Unannounced. Uninvited. Unwanted.

No, maybe not entirely unwanted.

He shouldn't have kissed her. Why he'd done it, he couldn't say. She'd looked so good, standing there, this beautiful vision from his past . . .

"Get a grip," he chided himself. "Like there aren't enough babes lying around?"

Actually, at that moment, there weren't. The closest blanket was smothered by a fish-belly-white old couple. Still, a lifeguard didn't generally have a hard time meeting girls.

But Kate hadn't been one of the endless parade of beach bims. She was not a bimbo—no, definitely not. Of course, that had been part of the problem. Because in their relationship, *he'd* been the bimbo. He was the one who'd decided to drop out of high school after his junior year. He was the one who hadn't mapped out every last detail of the rest of his life. Kate knew what she was doing in the world. Hell, she'd probably already picked out a retirement condo in Florida. And the one thing she'd made clear was that he didn't figure in the master plan.

No surprise, really. Kate was going to be someone. She had a full academic scholarship to one of the best colleges in the country. She wanted to get her law degree, save the environment, and become the first woman president— and that was just for openers.

And Justin? Justin just wanted to finish rebuilding his old sailboat and hit the water for parts unknown. Not exactly ambitious, but hey, who gave a damn about ambition? He knew plenty of ambitious people. Plenty of successful people. But the people he knew who were content with their lives, well, he could count them on the fingers of one hand.

He'd tried to explain this to Kate, but she hadn't seemed to understand. As far as she was concerned, he was just a summertime fling and nothing more. The beach bum she'd made it with—*almost* made it with—over summer vacation. Great story for her to tell all the other sub-urban snots at her next slumber party.

"I don't suppose you have any suntan oil, do you?"

Justin glanced to his right. About ten feet away, two girls in thong bikinis were staking their claim, carefully spreading their towels and ar-ranging their sun worshipping paraphernalia: cassette player, thick paperbacks, diet colas.

"Sorry," Justin said with a shrug, turning back to the water. They were regulars. A lot of guards had them. A perk that went with the job.

That's not why he loved guarding, though. He did this because when he was near the water, everything seemed simpler. Because he'd found a job where some suckers paid him to do what he'd do for free.

And it mattered, what he did. He saved peo-ple's lives. Last summer alone, he'd had sixteen saves. Not all of them had been going down for the last count, of course. Some, like that kid he had his eye on, had just been pushing their luck.

There was nothing like that feeling of pull-ing someone in, that look of gratitude on their face that said you were practically a god. He knew himself well enough to know that was part of the rush. But mostly, finally, he was a guard because of the water. That great, cold, dangerous place where he felt most at home.

That much, at least, Kate had understood about him. Kate, who was all light and sun and air, who'd loved the ocean as much as he did. He smiled, remembering one hot August night when they'd gone skinny-dipping. She was a strong swimmer, almost as strong as he was, and they'd gone out way too far, neither of them willing to stop. At last they did, floating silently side by side, their bodies just barely touching. The water was black and still and held the stars like a mirror. If he could have stayed there with her forever, he would have.

"Hey, Garrett. You awake up there?"

Luis Salgado. His boss. The lieutenant in this busiest sector of the beach. Justin recognized the voice instantly. He would have heard the Chevy Blazer coming if he hadn't been daydreaming. "Yeah, I'm awake, Lou."

Luis laughed. "Funny, I could have sworn you were zoning out. What's happening?"

"Nada. Except I got a kid on a boogie board who's getting a little out of his depth. I tried to whistle him in, but the surf's too loud for him to hear."

Luis shaded his eyes and gazed off into the distance. "I see him."

"I don't sleep in the chair, Lou." Justin pulled

down his shades and rolled sideways in the chair to look at Luis. There was another guard with him, a guy Justin hadn't seen around before. He had the streaked blond hair, wide shoulders, and smooth body of a swimmer.

"You don't shave, either," Luis remarked. He was a stocky, darkly tanned man in his thirties, with a thick mat of chest hair and a vicious-looking semi-circular scar on his right side. A reminder of a great white with a bad attitude. Luis's standard joke was that the shark had just wanted a little Mexican food.

Justin felt the stubble on his chin. "Had a little situation this morning," he explained.

"Situation, huh?" Luis grinned at the other guard. "He means a girl."

For once he's right, Justin thought.

"Hey, this is Alec Daniels. He's new."

Justin extended his hand and Alec shook it firmly.

"Justin's been with us for a month now," Luis explained. "He's a local, so he started before the main season hit. Plus he worked part-time last season. He'll show you the ropes."

"Man, Lou, I'm really not in the mood to break in a rookie this morning," Justin complained. "No offense to you, Alex."

"Alec. No X. Just a C."

"I knew I could count on you to be helpful as always, Garrett," Luis remarked, undaunted.

"Lou, if I'm such a pain, why are you getting me to play trainer?"

Luis stared up at Justin for a long moment. "How come you're watching the kid on the boogie board?"

"Because he looks like a kid who's getting himself in trouble. He's glancing around every two seconds. He flinched when a little splash caught him. He paddles like he's in too big a hurry. All of which means he's scared, but he doesn't want to look like a wuss, so he's forcing himself to go farther out." Justin paused to scan his two hundred meters of shoreline. Ten seconds left, ten seconds to the right, just like the training films had said. "People who are scared usually have a good reason to be scared."

Luis grinned. "See, Alec? That's why I'm putting you with Justin. He has no respect for authority, he's rude to people on the beach, he can't even bother to shave, but he's got the eye." Luis tapped his forefinger to the side of his head. "He's got the eye."

Luis took off in his Blazer, leaving Justin in an uncomfortable silence with Alec. "So. Can you swim?" Justin asked at last.

"I came in first in the last round of lifeguard

tryouts," Alec said. "And I was All-American in high school."

"Great. Then I think you'd better go for a swim right about now."

"Where to?"

Justin pointed. "That dumb-ass kid is getting caught in the current. He's on his way to Cape Cod. In about twenty seconds he's going to realize that, and then he's going to freak."

Alec nodded. "I got it." He took off down the beach.

"Hey, rookie! Your buoy, man." Justin lifted the red plastic float by its rope and slung it toward Alec. "Never go without your buoy."

Alec slipped the nylon rope over his shoulder and neck. "It's Alec. Not rookie," he said, before turning and dashing into the surf. As soon as he was knee-deep, he dove neatly into the water and began powering his way out toward the boy.

Justin watched him go and found himself chuckling for the first time that morning. "Well," he muttered, "at least the rookie can swim."

Six

"Told you you should have worn your suit," Chelsea said. She peeled off her paint-spattered T-shirt to reveal a brand-new, red two-piece bathing suit. It left very little to the imagination. Neon-red mirrored shades and matching hoop earrings completed the look.

"Nice suit," Kate said.

Chelsea kicked off her sandals and dropped onto the hot sand next to Kate. "What?" she pressed. "You don't really like it, do you? It's too much, isn't it? I look like one of those Slim-Fast *before* pictures, don't I?" She fell back onto the sand with a dramatic sigh. "I am a pig. I am a walrus. I am a beached whale."

"You look incredible," Kate assured her. Kate had been listening to Chelsea's body insecurities for years. Chelsea had plenty of curves and, according to every weight chart ever made, was exactly the right weight for her height, but that didn't stop her from obsessing. "Really."

"I'm sorry." Chelsea sat up. "I'm being a jerk. You're in the middle of a major romantic trauma, and I'm counting my cellulite lumps. So tell me already."

Kate stretched out her legs and began to scoop sand over them. The heavy warmth of the sand was somehow reassuring. So was the idea of being buried alive.

She closed her eyes and turned her face to the sun.

The sounds around her were reassuring too. The ocean was in a gentle mood this morning, coming and going like the rush of the wind through leaves. Behind her, the manic tunes from a video arcade caught on the breeze and came to her in little high-pitched fragments.

"I'm starving again," Chelsea murmured, as the sweet smell of caramel corn wafted by on the breeze. "Do you think that candy apple I ate counted as a fruit or a fat?"

"Chelsea, you don't need to diet."

"Maybe you're right," Chelsea agreed. "After all, the most beautiful specimen of African-American maleness I have ever seen just happens to be giving me the eye." She nodded her head toward the rowdy co-ed volleyball game in progress a few yards down the beach. "I think it is a sign of my supreme loyalty and best friendship that I am ignoring those incredible buns." She lowered her sunglasses to get a better look. "And why am I ignoring them? Because you are about to tell me something you probably should have told me a long time ago, and I, being the world's best best friend, am going to give you the benefit of my wisdom and insight."

The object of Chelsea's interest aced his serve. She gave him an appreciative yell, and he gave her an appreciative smile. Then, all business, Chelsea turned back to Kate. "Any time, Kate. We've already spent an hour wandering around the boardwalk in total silence and a half hour making sure we picked a spot on the beach that was nowhere near Justin's lifeguard chair. It's getting old."

Kate didn't answer. She knew Chelsea meant well, but she just didn't want to discuss it. Not now, not later, not ever.

"Okay." Chelsea pushed a sand crab away with her toe. "Let me take a stab at this. This Justin dude is the 'nothing little flirtation' you told me about from last summer. The insignificant diversion you didn't want to go into any detail over because it was really just too boring."

She gave Kate a scathing look. "And you claim you always tell me everything."

"There wasn't much to tell," Kate lied.

"Sell that somewhere else," Chelsea said. "Something major went on between you and this Justin guy. And who could blame you? I mean, those *eyes,* Kate!"

Kate didn't want to talk about Justin's eyes. She remembered them all too well. Deep-blue in sunlight, near-green in moonlight. And when he was angry, as he'd been that last day, a dark, stormy gray. "I'd rather not go into it all," she said softly.

"You have to. You can't ignore this guy. He showers in our bathroom."

"That's why I want to move out."

"We'll get to that. First things first—the juicy details." She glanced over at Mr. Volleyball one more time. "Details you should have told me last summer when they were still fresh in your memory."

They were still fresh, Kate knew. She'd hoped they would all fade. She'd tried to think of them as memories that over time would come to be nothing more than a wistful story of a summer infatuation. But that hadn't happened. "I'm really sorry, Chelsea," Kate said softly. "If it helps any, it's the *only* thing I've never told you."

"But why?"

Kate tried to stare out at the waves, but her tears made it impossible. She was glad she had on sunglasses. "I guess—" She shrugged helplessly. "I don't know, because he hurt me."

"But you could have told me that. We could have had an all-night munchathon, gone through a couple boxes of Kleenex—the usual stuff you do for me when I get dumped."

"I was . . . embarrassed, I guess."

"Ah." Chelsea nodded. "I thought so. The great Kate Quinn is always the dumper, not the dumpee."

"It's not that," Kate said angrily. "I thought . . . I actually thought he was the one, Chelsea. It was different with Justin. It was so *intense*, you know?"

"I know." Chelsea shrugged. "Or maybe I don't. I think every guy's the one. You know me—I'm not very discriminating."

Kate managed a smile. It was true. Chelsea fell in love easily and often. And every single time, she was certain this one was *forever*.

"So what happened, exactly?" Chelsea pressed.

Kate sighed. She was in this deep. She might as well get it over with. "My family had their usual cottage all of August, remember? Justin was lifeguarding, and we met on the beach, and well, you know, one thing led to et cetera, et cetera."

"Don't skip the et ceteras. That's my favorite part."

Kate closed her eyes and let the feelings come back, just for a moment. "We just connected. I've never met anyone like him, Chels. He's incredibly intense, and incredibly smart, and incredibly *different*."

"You forgot incredibly gorgeous."

Kate opened her eyes. "But he's frustrating, too. He quit school after his junior year because he thought it was a waste of time. Can you believe it? He said he was bored."

"Actually, I can see his point. . . ."

"Of course, my parents really freaked when they discovered I was dating a dropout."

"That *would* freak your parents out. Come to think of it, it'd freak mine out too." She laughed. "That's why they like Greg. They think he's too good for me, and of course Greg agrees. But enough about my relatively boring love life. Am I just being dense? You fell in love with a great guy and he fell in love with you. So what's the problem?"

"The problem was that Justin doesn't know what he wants, except that he doesn't want to be tied down to any one person. And when it looked like I might turn out to be that one person, he just—" She choked on something that felt dangerously like a sob. "Let's just say he made it clear what his priorities were, and I wasn't on the list."

Chelsea cocked her head to one side. "How did you know this, exactly?"

"I just did, okay?"

"Not okay."

Kate bit her lip. "Trust me. I had plenty of evidence."

"In my book, he's innocent until proven guilty. Especially with eyes like those." She leaned closer. "Tell me, Kate."

"Look, we had this really hot and heavy night, okay?"

"Wait a minute! You—"

"No, I didn't. But I thought about it. A lot." She laughed ruefully. "I thought about it constantly, if you want to know the truth." Kate sighed. "And I decided that things were getting too intense, without us knowing where we were going. I wanted to back off a little, cool things down, you know?"

"So what happened?"

"We had this fight, this stupid fight about commitment. The next morning, I felt really lousy. So I bought him a box of chocolates. He's like me—he has a thing for chocolate."

"Well, sure." Chelsea grinned. "It's an aphrodisiac."

"While he was at work, I went down to the marina where he kept his boat, to leave the chocolates with an apology note. He'd just bought this boat, this rickety piece of junk he thinks he's going to sail off into the sunset, and he was all excited about it. So anyway, I go there and I find there's *already* a note. On a pillow inside the cabin. Guess what it said."

"Uh-oh. Was it on pink scented stationery, by any chance?"

"Lined notebook paper, actually." Kate knew the message by heart. "It said, 'Thanks for another beautiful night. You're an amazing lover, but then you always have been. Racey.'" She sneered. "I can guess how she got her nickname."

"Look out!"

The shouted warning came too late. The volleyball landed in Chelsea's lap, sending sand flying. Chelsea yelped in surprise.

"Sorry," said Mr. Volleyball, reaching down for the ball. "I should have caught that."

"No problem," Chelsea said. He grinned and ran back to his game.

"That is so disappointing," Chelsea lamented.

"That body, and he has a voice like PeeWee Herman? There goes the fantasy." She shrugged. "So anyway, back to this note. Did it occur to you that maybe it was an old letter? It could have belonged to the boat's former owner."

"I don't think so."

"Why?"

Kate was unable to keep the bitterness out of her voice. "Because they left some other evidence."

"What kind of—" Chelsea's eyes went wide. "Eww. You don't mean a what-I-think-you-mean, do you?"

"Let me put it this way—at least it was *safe* sex."

Chelsea whistled. "Okay, great eyes or not, I'm willing to admit he's a toad. Did you see him again after that?"

"Once. We fought, he said he wasn't ready to commit, that he'd never made any promises . . . you know the rest."

"How did he explain the—you know—evidence?"

"He didn't. I never got around to telling him that I saw it. Why listen to a bunch of lame excuses? Besides, we were too busy fighting about us for me to worry about . . . her."

"You must have known you'd run into him this summer."

"I thought it was safe to come back to O.C. His mom had just remarried at the end of last summer, and they were moving to Vermont. I figured he was long gone. Anyway, you see now why we have to move." Kate heaved a sigh. "Besides, I'd managed to brainwash myself into believing it was all no big deal. Then, this morning . . ."

For a while Chelsea let Kate's silence alone. Then she reached over and squeezed Kate's arm. "Look, I *have* to say this, okay?"

"Could I possibly stop you?"

"It's just that it's obvious there's still something going on there between you and Justin. You know. What's the phrase? *Unfinished business.*"

"Yeah, you're right," Kate agreed grimly. "I never really told him what an unmitigated bastard I think he is."

Chelsea laughed. "Only you would combine the words 'unmitigated' and 'bastard' in the same sentence."

Kate sat up and began brushing the sand off her legs. "We've got to find people to take over our lease as soon as possible, Chelsea. Today, if we can. I'm not spending another night in that house unless I absolutely have to."

"You absolutely have to. There's no way we're going to find anyone that quickly."

"Who knows? Maybe someone's responded to our signs already. That Irish guy did." This was good. This made sense. She'd get out of the house and get Justin out of her life once and for all. "Come on," Kate said. "Let's get to work."

Chelsea stood reluctantly and sighed. "Did you ever think that maybe Justin's living in the boathouse is some kind of karma thing? You know—fate? Like our losing the cottage and finding the house. Part of some cosmic plan to get the two of you back together? Maybe it's meant to be. Maybe it's meta—"

"No, Chelsea, it is *not* metaphysically correct," Kate said as she started across the sand. "And it isn't karma. It's just a mistake I made once that I don't intend to make again."

SEVEN

Grace stood in front of the huge window that wrapped clear around the penthouse living room on three sides. From fourteen floors up, you could see the entire length of Ocean City, down the rows of condominiums, past the hotels and motels and the shabby wood-frame structures in the south end, all the way to the amusement-park rides, turning and glittering at the limit of her vision.

The beach below was dotted here and there with the hardy souls who got out early for their day in the sun. A pair of surfers tried vainly to catch a swell big enough to ride. Far, far out, the ocean simply disappeared into a vague, indistinct line between sea and sky.

The little airplane that towed advertisement banners past the beach floated by at eye level.

The banner read CAPTAIN TONY'S—O.C.'S BEST SEAFOOD. Grace always enjoyed watching the little plane. She waved to the pilot as he drifted past, but she knew the tinted windows of the condo rendered her invisible.

Better enjoy it one last time, Grace told herself. She sipped at her coffee. It was wonderful, of course. Much better than the stuff they served at The Claw. But then, her mother had good taste. You had to say that for her. This was Jamaican Blue Mountain, forty bucks a pound. And the machine in the kitchen had ground it fresh, then brewed it with spring water.

Yes, there would be plenty to miss about life with Mother.

Grace drifted to the south side of the condo, a window that aimed straight along the length of Ocean City. This condo was definitely north end. When she found her own place, it would definitely be south end. No more panoramic views. No more plush carpet and designer furniture. No more whirlpool bath when the day was over. She'd been in some of the south-end furnished rentals. They all seemed to have the same bright yellow vinyl couches and cracked linoleum floors.

Grace gazed across the bay and took another sip of coffee. In the distance she could make out the mainland, with its marshes and scruffy forests. It wasn't as dramatic as the ocean view, or as lively and fascinating as the view down the length of Ocean City, but it was the view Grace preferred—because it showed the road that led *away* from Ocean City.

"You're up early."

Grace tensed at the sound of her mother's voice, but she didn't look away from the distant causeway. "Yes, I am."

"You didn't get home from work last night till after one," her mother said. "And here you are not only up, but dressed by ten?"

"I'm surprised you remember. You were . . . not entirely coherent." She turned slowly, tearing her gaze away from the few tiny, distant cars that were leaving Ocean City.

Elegant as always, Ellen Caywood wore a beige silk dressing gown and gold slippers. Her ash-blond hair—Clairol #9—was already combed into a neat French twist. Her lipstick was expertly applied. Grace had rarely seen her without a layer or two of Lancome.

Ellen took a sip from her own mug. "Thanks for making the coffee," she said. "You're never up before me. I didn't even know you could operate the machine. It must be one of the many vitally important skills you've picked up working in that dive."

"I'm leaving, Mother," Grace said suddenly.

"The job?"

"You."

"What on earth are you talking about?"

"I'm getting a place of my own," Grace explained.

Ellen pursed her lips. "You don't have any money."

"I have a job, remember? Last night I took home fifty-two dollars in tips. Saturday I made twice that."

Her mother rolled her eyes. "That kind of money won't keep that precious car of yours in gas, let alone pay rent."

Grace nodded slightly. "Then I guess you have nothing to worry about, do you? I'll come running home with my tail between my legs and beg you to take care of me."

"I won't allow it," Ellen snapped.

"I'm eighteen, Mother. Of legal age. You may remember I had a birthday a few weeks back. We celebrated it in grand style. You got drunk with Darryl, and just before you passed out, you slipped me a hundred-dollar bill and told me to go buy myself something nice. Then"—Grace looked away, struggling to keep her voice hard—"as a bonus gift, Darryl tried to grope me."

"That's a lie!"

"I was sitting on the couch. He stood behind me, slid his hand down the front of my shirt, and said, 'You're legal now.' He seemed to think that was quite a witty thing to say."

Ellen took a deep swallow of her coffee—or was it brandy? She looked at Grace with cold, suspicious eyes. "You want out, go. Get out now. But when you do come crawling back, and you will, there will be a new set of rules, young lady. I've let you get away with too much for too long."

A movement behind her mother drew Grace's attention. It was Bo, wearing a pair of long, baggy shorts and a black T-shirt with several artfully torn holes. He took in the scene with a barely visible nod.

"What's up, Gracie?"

"I'm moving out, Bo." For the first time, her voice quavered. Moving out on her mother might be an act of liberation, but leaving Bo felt a lot like betrayal. He was years away from being able to do what she was doing. Years away from his own freedom.

Bo nodded and clenched his right hand into a fist. "Need some help with your stuff?"

"I'd like that," Grace whispered.

She had already packed two suitcases and filled three small boxes with her personal things. While she and Bo carried them out to the elevator in the hallway, Ellen disappeared into her bedroom. Grace couldn't be sure whether her mother was sad to see her leave, or angry, or even relieved. She did know, though, there would be no big scene, no low-class shouting match to wake up the neighbors. Ellen Caywood would never let the mask fall like that.

Grace and Bo rode the elevator down in silence. Her two-year-old royal-blue Mazda Miata was parked at the curb. Grace tossed Bo the keys. He liked to start her car and put the top down.

When everything was loaded, Bo stood awkwardly beside her, his hands jammed in his pockets. "So, you got a place?"

"Not yet. But I have some leads. I'll let you know as soon as I have a phone number. In the meantime, if you need me, you can always leave a message at The Claw, okay?"

Bo kicked at a piece of gravel on the sidewalk. "It'll be cool being on your own. Won't have to deal with her." Bo jerked his head in the direction of their penthouse. "Plus, no annoying little brother." He gave her a crooked smile.

Grace put her arms around Bo and squeezed him to her tightly. "I love my annoying little brother. And you'd better understand one thing— any place of mine is yours, too. Got that?"

Bo nodded, then disengaged himself from her grasp. "Let's not get all weepy," he said.

Grace shoved him playfully. "Take care of yourself, all right? I won't be far away."

"Cool." Bo nodded. His eyes were glistening. Grace climbed into the car. Bo waved, and she waved back.

"I'm sorry, Bo," she whispered very softly. Then she pulled the little sports car through a tight U-turn and sped away.

"So what's your name?" Chelsea asked, trying her best to sound as if she cared. It was late afternoon and the roommate interviews were beginning to blur together like a bad party that refused to end.

"Chrissy," the girl replied, shifting on the old brown couch with the bad spring. She crossed, then uncrossed her legs. Then she crossed them again.

Chelsea nodded. "Chrissy." She glanced at Kate, hoping for some backup. Kate made a don't-look-at-me face. She'd conducted the last three interviews, and she'd made it clear that this one was all Chelsea's.

"So, Chrissy," Chelsea began. "The rent's two hundred and seventy-five dollars a month. Plus electricity and phone, of course. Can you afford that much?"

"How much?" Chrissy asked, looking a little confused.

"Two seventy-five, plus your share of however much electricity and phone are," Chelsea repeated.

"I think I may get this job, you know, on the boardwalk, making funnel cakes. And it pays pretty good."

"How many hours will you be working?" Chelsea asked.

"I don't have the job yet, but I think maybe the manager will hire me. He said I have a cute smile."

"Do you have any money to pay the rent right now?" Chelsea pressed.

"I have twenty-eight dollars, but I have to buy this great shirt I saw," Chrissy replied. Then she added, "The shirt costs twenty."

"So after that, you'll have eight dollars," Chelsea summarized.

"The rent is two seventy-five," Kate pointed out.

"I may get this job making funnel cakes."

"On the boardwalk. Yes, we know." Chelsea sighed.

Kate stood and nodded toward the door. "We'll let you know, Chrissy," she said.

Chelsea stood too. Chrissy was a little slow to

get the message. But then Chrissy seemed like the kind of girl who was slow to get pretty much everything.

Finally, when Kate held open the front door, Chrissy caught on. "How are you going to let me know?" she asked as she headed for the door. "I mean, I'm staying with my folks in their camper. There's no phone or anything."

"Don't worry," Chelsea said with a vague wave. "We'll just light up the bat signal."

The next two interviews were no better. The first girl promised she'd be able to get the rent together within a month or two at the most. The second explained that she'd soon be making really big money, "if you know what I mean." She said "if you know what I mean" often enough that Kate and Chelsea began to suspect they *did* know what she meant.

"So far we're doing really well," Chelsea remarked as she closed the door on the last applicant. "We just put our notices up last night, and already we've had a lot of responses. Unfortunately, the responses we're getting are from morons, psychos, and drug dealers."

"Maybe we shouldn't be so picky," Kate said. "After all, we're getting out of this house once we have enough people to cover the lease and pay us back our deposit."

Chelsea arched her brows. "It may take us a week, even two, to get all the people we need and find another place."

"It *can't* take that long," Kate said.

"You tell me which of the people we've interviewed we would want to live with for a week. Or even for a day."

Kate jumped up and began pacing back and forth in front of the couch. "I know, I know, but I've got to get out of here, Chels," she said. "Is there anyone else waiting out on the porch?"

Chelsea got up to look. The porch was empty, but someone was pulling up in a shiny, new-looking blue sports car. She stuck her head back inside and whispered, "Hey, I think we have a hot prospect here."

A slim, graceful girl emerged from the car. Her dark, thick hair was styled in a shoulder-length cut. High cheekbones and full lips gave her an exotic, sexy look. It was hard to tell if she was older than they were, or if she'd just figured out how to *look* older than they were.

"I've seen her somewhere, I think," Chelsea said.

Kate stared out the window. "She looks like she has money." The girl paused long enough to look down toward the boathouse. When she turned back to mount the steps, she was smiling slightly.

Chelsea held open the screen door. "You here about the roommate opening?"

"Yes, I am. My name is Grace Caywood."

"I'm Chelsea Lennox, and that's Kate Quinn." Chelsea nodded toward the couch. "Come on in and let's talk. Watch that spring in the middle cushion, by the way. It's deadly."

Grace smiled neutrally and made herself comfortable on the couch. She took the room in with a sweep of her almond-shaped green eyes.

"First, I guess we'd better tell you that the rent is two seventy-five a month—plus the electricity and phone bills, of course." Chelsea waited for a reaction from Grace. She half expected her to sneer at the amount. After all, the girl was wearing more than two seventy-five in jewelry alone. But Grace simply closed, then opened her eyes, a gesture that Chelsea took to be acknowledgment.

"You can pay that?" Kate pressed.

"That won't be a problem."

Kate smiled. "May I ask if you have a job?"

"You may. And the answer is yes, I do. I'm a waitress at The Claw."

"That's why you seem familiar," Chelsea exclaimed, snapping her fingers. "We were there last night."

Grace nodded. "You came in to get change. I saw you again when you came in to post your notice on the bulletin board by the phone."

"Where are you from?" Chelsea asked.

"I'm from here. Ocean City. I've lived here all my life."

"But you're looking for a summer rental?" Kate asked doubtfully.

"I've just moved out of my mother's place."

"Just?" Chelsea echoed.

"Just. As in this morning."

Chelsea and Kate exchanged a glance.

"Maybe I can make this easier for you," Grace said. "I don't smoke, I don't have any annoying pets, I don't have any contagious diseases. More to the point"—she reached into her soft leather shoulder bag and pulled out her checkbook—"I have two hundred and seventy-five dollars."

"Excuse us while we have a brief conference," Chelsea said, pulling Kate to her feet and leading her into the dining room.

"I say yes," she whispered when they were safely out of earshot.

Kate gazed back toward the living room, frowning. "She just moved out of her mom's house this morning. I wonder what that's all about."

"She has my vote. She's the first person we've gotten who has the money and seems to have earned it by honest means. Besides, you don't really care. We're moving out, remember?"

"All right," Kate agreed. "It's unanimous, then."

They headed back into the living room. "Grace, we'd love to have you as our house-mate," Chelsea announced.

Grace gave them the same noncommittal smile. "Where would my bedroom be?"

Chelsea shrugged. "We have five bedrooms total. Four are upstairs, one downstairs. I guess you can take your pick. You're the first to choose."

"Haven't you two decided?"

"We want to stay flexible," Kate said quickly. "You know, so that everyone's happy."

Only a slight narrowing of Grace's eyes indicated that she doubted the story. "Very thoughtful," she said. "How long is this lease for, by the way? Is this strictly a summer rental?"

"I suppose Mr. Mabrey might rent it for the winter," Chelsea replied. "I didn't really ask him."

"I assume you two are off to college in the fall?" Grace asked as she pulled a pen out of her wallet.

"We're both heading to Columbia," Chelsea answered. "I'll be studying art. Kate will be attending the prestigious School of Taking Over the World."

83

"So this is a warmup drill, of sorts? To see if you can stand each other?"

"We've been best friends since sixth grade," Kate replied, "and we've never fought."

Chelsea nodded sincerely. She managed to keep from bursting into laughter for all of about five seconds.

"Okay," Kate admitted. "We've had our disagreements, once or twice. But not this summer."

Grace gave them her same cool smile. "People always say that when they get to a tourist town like O.C. They think they're in some special place that protects them from the real world. Then they find out it's just like home, with a little more sand." She tore off a check. "Whom shall I make this out to?"

"Kate Quinn," Kate answered. "We've already paid the rent for the month."

"She handles the money," Chelsea said. "I can't be trusted with cash." She was gratified to see Grace smile at the joke. At least the girl had a sense of humor. That was always a good sign. "So, what are your plans for the fall?" Chelsea asked.

Grace filled out the check and handed it to Kate. "I've got a couple Ivy League schools in mind. Nothing definite."

"You mean you haven't heard whether they've accepted you or not?" Kate asked.

"Oh, I've heard." Grace returned her checkbook to her purse. "And they have." She gave a little shrug. "I'm just not sure if I care."

For a moment nobody spoke.

"Well, I guess you should go ahead and help yourself to a bedroom," Chelsea said at last. "The downstairs bedroom is right around the corner. The upstairs bedrooms are—"

"Upstairs?" Grace offered.

"Why don't you go take a look?" Chelsea suggested.

"I think I'll do that."

As she passed the dining room, Grace paused to gaze out the window. "Anything wrong?" Chelsea asked.

"I was just admiring the boathouse."

"Some guy lives there," Chelsea explained, "but not to worry. He has kitchen and bath privileges, but we hardly ever see him."

"Too bad," Grace said.

"What did she mean by that, I wonder?" Kate asked as Grace disappeared up the stairs.

"I think she was trying to be funny," Chelsea said. She frowned. "I hope she doesn't take the bedroom I wanted."

"It doesn't matter, Chelsea. We're not staying."

"Shouldn't we have told *her* that?"

"There's no need to get everyone involved in all the details of our lives. How am I supposed to explain to a perfect stranger why I can't stay here?"

"You have a point there. I'm your best friend and *I* can't understand it."

"Shh. Here she comes."

Grace descended the stairs and rejoined them in the living room. "I'd like the downstairs bedroom, if that's all right. I work late, and that way I'm less likely to bother other people."

"Sure," Chelsea said. Another good sign, her being polite enough to worry about other people's sleep. Polite, and with a sense of humor.

"I did have one question, though," Grace continued. "You said I was the first person in the house, aside from the two of you?"

"You are," Kate confirmed.

"Well then, you may want to have a talk with the guy upstairs. He looks like he's pretty well moved in."

Chelsea blinked. "Guy upstairs?"

"Yeah. Some Irish guy. Said his name was Connor."

EIGHT

Kate reached the door first. "I hope you're decent in there, because I'm coming in," she announced, throwing the door open.

Connor looked up angrily from the book he was reading. "Who the hell do you think you are, barging into a man's room like this?"

"Who the hell do you think *you* are," Kate shot back, parroting his accent, "moving into this room to begin with? I thought you left this morning. Maybe I should just call the cops."

"Let's not get ourselves into an uproar," he said quietly. He crossed his arms over his chest. "Last I heard, you were convinced you couldn't live under the same roof with that shower fellow. What was his name? Justin?" He shrugged. "Of course, it's none of my affair, but he seemed nice enough to me. A little quiet for my taste, but at least he left me some hot water. Still, I figured since you were leaving, you wouldn't care if I moved in."

"Look," Kate said firmly. "A, my personal life is not really your business. And B, even if we wanted you for a housemate—and trust me, we don't—we can't have guys living in this house. Not even temporarily."

"Isn't that a bit sexist?"

"It's not that," Chelsea said. "It's just—" She paused. She wasn't quite sure *why* they hadn't considered having male housemates. They'd just automatically put "Female Housemates Needed" on their signs—not that it had stopped Connor from showing up.

Justin, of course, was a different story. He'd come with the house. And besides, he really lived in the boathouse. But as for having guys right down the hall—it seemed so, well, *real world.*

"I should think you'd like having a fellow around," Connor said. "I'm good for a few things. Heavy lifting, for example."

"And?" Chelsea prompted.

"I could always defend your honor—" He winked at her. "Assuming you want it defended."

Chelsea looked over at Kate. "We *could* let him stay, Kate," she suggested tentatively.

Kate leaned against the wall and groaned. "I

can just hear me explaining that one. *That's right, Mom, we're living with this Irish guy. How'd we meet him? Oh, well, it's really kind of a cute story. See, he broke into our house last night—*"

"This morning, actually," Connor corrected.

"Maybe Kate's right," Chelsea said. "My parents would have a major cow."

Connor didn't respond. He was busy unzipping his pillow. He began tearing out wads of fuzzy white stuffing and tossing them onto the bed.

Chelsea exchanged a nervous glance with Kate. "Um, Connor?" she inquired delicately. "Is there some reason you're yanking the guts out of your pillow?"

Connor reached deep into the pillow and extracted a crisp wad of bills. "Two seventy-five, wasn't that the sum in question?" he asked.

Neither girl answered. "I'll take that as a yes," Connor said as he began to count out the bills onto his sheet.

"Maybe you haven't heard," Kate said, shaking her head in disbelief. "We have these charming institutions here in the United States. We call them banks."

"Ah, but the bank of Riordan is open twenty-four hours a day," Connor said, patting his pillow affectionately.

"Where did you get that money? You do have a job, I hope?" Chelsea asked doubtfully.

"I assure you every Yankee dollar of this was earned by honest means. I make doughnuts."

The way he pronounced it, the word came out "doonuts." Chelsea laughed. "You make doughnuts?"

Connor held out the money. "I make doughnuts with my hands"—he nodded toward a rickety desk, where several sheets of paper lay in disarray—"but I make poetry with my soul."

"You want to be a writer?" Chelsea asked.

"I *am* a writer. I want to be a *published* writer."

Chelsea grabbed the cash out of Connor's hand. "He's a struggling *poet*, Kate," she whispered. "We can't throw a poet out on the street, can we? How could we live with ourselves?"

Kate looked skeptically at Connor. "He doesn't look dangerous," she admitted. "And since it's not like we're staying . . ."

Chelsea waved the money under Kate's nose. "Come on, take a whiff, Kate. That's the sweet smell of rent."

"I'm not so sure about having a guy in the house," Chelsea said as she entered the bedroom at the end of the hall where Kate was waiting for her. "There are whiskers in the bathroom sink. And I discovered the hard way that Connor left the toilet seat up."

Kate was sprawled on the unmade bed by the window. "Too late now," she said. "You're the sucker who fell for his struggling-poet routine."

"He is kind of charming." Chelsea sank onto the bed next to Kate. "Don't you just love that accent?"

"What I love is his two seventy-five. The sooner we're out of here, the better." She smiled grimly. "And it *better* be sooner. My parents would hemorrhage if they found out I was living with a guy. "

"You know, I'm seeing a whole new side of you, Kate. You're acting downright ruthless."

"Independence is bringing out the worst in me." Kate sighed. Boy, she was beat. She hadn't been this tired since she'd pulled an all-nighter for her physics final.

"Well, I'm glad you let him stay. I kind of like the guy. Besides, maybe he'll bring home free doughnuts." Chelsea dusted off the headboard with the palm of her hand. "You know, if we *were* staying here, I wouldn't want this room."

"Why not? It has the bay window, and it's right next to the bathroom."

"It's way too small. And it has the only single bed in the house."

"The bed is plenty big for me," Kate said.

"Are you *sure*?" Chelsea asked with a leer.

"Chels, look me right in the eyes," Kate commanded. "I'm telling the truth when I say it's over between Justin and I."

"Me," Chelsea corrected. "Justin and me."

"No, it's *I*," Kate argued. She frowned. "Wait a minute, don't try to distract me. I'm telling you, that's all in the past. Over. Done."

"So why do you have to move out? If it really were ancient history, you wouldn't be so anxious to bail out of here, and you sure wouldn't be afraid to even talk to Justin."

"I am not afraid."

"Yes you are, and it's not like you, Kate," Chelsea pointed out. "I mean, *this* is the Kate Quinn who went skydiving last spring? *This* is the Kate Quinn who thinks crossing Antarctica by dogsled sounds like fun?" Chelsea shook her head and smiled her most infuriating grin. "All Justin had to do was walk out of the shower wearing that towel and you went into brain-lock. If he'd said, *Kate, I still love you, I want you, come on down to my boathouse so I can show you my mast—*"

"Chelsea!" Kate slugged her in the arm.

"As I was saying, you'd have picked right up where you left off."

"You are dead wrong. Not to mention being more than a little juvenile."

"You're the one who wants to run away just because your old boyfriend happens to show up. Does that remind you of something?" Chelsea challenged. "For example, the time Dwayne Torricelli kissed you on the cheek in sixth grade and you decided you had to move to another school district?"

Suddenly Chelsea smiled, and Kate turned to follow the direction of her gaze. The front yard, the bay . . . the *boathouse.* "What did you see?" Kate demanded.

Chelsea made an innocent face and raised her hands. "Nothing."

But the sound of the front door closing downstairs betrayed the truth. "It's him, isn't it?" Kate snapped as her heart went into high gear.

"Who?" Chelsea asked. "The guy who doesn't worry you?"

"Shh!"

They heard a heavy male tread on the stairs.

Suddenly, as if he had materialized from thin air, Justin was standing in the doorway to the bedroom. He was wearing jeans and a faded denim shirt with the sleeves rolled up.

"Listen," he began, "I just needed to find something out."

"Excuse me, I have stuff to do," Chelsea said quickly, ducking toward the exit. "Vital stuff in another state. Maybe even another country. Catch you later."

But Justin didn't move. "This isn't personal or anything. I just need to know about the phone."

"What about the phone?" Kate asked, forcing herself to meet his eyes.

"Do you have one?"

"No."

"Are you getting one?" he asked.

"Yes. They said they could hook us up tomorrow."

"When you get it, I want to use it. I'll help pay the bill. My boss has been ragging me to get a phone so he can call me in for overtime."

"That would be fine," Kate replied.

Chelsea rolled her eyes, then reached out and lifted Justin's arm from the doorjamb and slid past him.

"Well, that's all I wanted to know," Justin said. Still, he didn't make a move to leave.

Say something, you idiot, Kate thought frantically. *Don't let him think he's having an effect on you.* "Um, we're not staying," Kate blurted. "I mean, Chelsea and I. Me. I. We're just getting the phone in so we can interview roommates by phone. And so our parents can call, you know."

Way to go, Kate. Now you're babbling.

A shadow of a smile passed over Justin's lips. "Running away?"

"We don't like the house."

"Bull."

"I know what you think," Kate said shakily.

"Do you?"

"You think it's because of you."

"I know it's because of me," Justin said.

"You know, Justin," Kate said, making her voice hard, "the whole world does not revolve around you."

Justin nodded. "No, it doesn't. You made that very clear last summer."

"Me?" Kate practically choked on her rage. "I'm not the one who—" She closed her eyes. What was she doing? They'd already had this fight.

"I'm not going to do this," she whispered. "We already know how it ends."

Justin seemed ready to argue, to try to say something that would make everything all right between them. But after a moment he just shrugged. He looked out the window, attempted a smile, and failed.

"You're right," he said. "We know how it ends." Without another word he turned and headed away down the hall.

"You told me you loved me," Kate whispered.

She hadn't meant for him to hear, but suddenly his footsteps in the hallway stopped. In a muffled voice he spoke two words. Then he headed down the steps, closing the front door of the house softly behind him.

Two words. *I did.* Putting an end to what Chelsea had called "unfinished business."

Or had the words been *I do*?

NINE

"Are you awake?" Chelsea whispered. It was early the next morning—too early, if you asked Chelsea.

"I am now," Kate grumbled, twisting in her sheets. "Is something the matter?"

"Bad architectural design. The only way into this bathroom is through your room. Connor's got his boy things in the other upstairs bathroom—razors and shaving cream and stuff—and I sort of figured the downstairs bathroom would be for Grace. And Justin."

Kate rubbed her eyes. "Whatever."

"But if I share this bath with you, I'll have to come through your room every time I want to use it."

"No big deal. I mean, it's not like we're staying here for long." Kate yawned. "What are you doing up already?"

"Job hunting. The next time you see me, I'll be gainfully employed. I hope."

"I'm impressed."

"You thought I'd just wait till I got desperate, then call home and bum some cash off my parents, didn't you?"

"Chels," Kate said sincerely, "*you* may underestimate yourself. But I never do."

Chelsea fingered the carefully ironed khaki shorts hanging off Kate's closet door. "You broke down and actually used an iron? I'm sure the folks at Safe Seas will be impressed. Nervous?"

"Not too." Kate hesitated. "Well, actually, yes. First-day jitters."

"I hope I can have some of those soon."

Chelsea took a leisurely shower and dried her hair. She was just putting the finishing touches on her mascara when Kate pounded on the door. "I have to get to work this morning, you know," she called. "I'm supposed to be there by eight thirty, and it's already seven twenty."

Chelsea opened the door. "I had to get pretty. And I do look good, don't I?" Kate rolled her eyes in answer. "By the way," Chelsea added as she left, "I think we're out of hot water."

She headed downstairs, listening to the sounds the household made as it slowly came alive—the shower running upstairs, the ringing alarm clock, the bustling in the kitchen downstairs. The sounds weren't so different from the ones she'd woken up to all her life, except that this wasn't her parents' house. That wasn't her dad running the shower, and her big brother swatting at his alarm clock, and her mom grabbing a quick breakfast before going off to work.

This was *her* house. She paid the rent. She decided for herself when to get up and when to go to sleep. She would make her own breakfast, with food she'd bought with her own money.

Food. Oh, right . . . *food.*

She and Kate had completely forgotten. Last night they'd just munched some fries on the boardwalk. But neither of them had thought to hit a grocery store.

Justin was in the kitchen, sitting on the counter as he spooned up half a cantaloupe. He had on his red lifeguard trunks and a white T-shirt. A big, tan, short-haired dog was eating from a dish on the floor.

Suddenly the words Kate had quoted from the letter she'd found in Justin's boat came back to Chelsea. *You're an amazing lover, but then you always have been.* It was hard to block out information like that.

"Hi," Chelsea said. "I'm Chelsea. I guess

we've never been properly introduced. I'm a friend of Kate's."

Justin nodded. "Kate told me about you. You know, back—" He hesitated.

"Back when you two were going out?"

"Yeah." He pointed at the dog. "Meet Mooch."

"Hi, Mooch." The dog kept eating, loudly and enthusiastically.

"I'm done, Justin."

Chelsea spun around, startled. A blond guy wandered in from the hallway. He was wearing red swim trunks too. "Shower's all yours," he said as he toweled off his chest.

Chelsea couldn't help staring. There was definitely something familiar about him.

The guy laughed. "You're the girl on the bridge. The girl who bummed a toilet. My name's Alec."

Chelsea snapped her fingers. "The guy in the Jeep!" She rolled her eyes. "I'm Chelsea, although you can call me by my Native American name, *Pees in Winnebagos.*"

Alec laughed.

"Where are you staying, Alec?" She couldn't help but look at him. Not that he was sexy, really. It was more that he had one of those perfect male bodies she'd seen in art class when they studied Greek statues. Perfect, chiseled proportions.

"I camped out in my tent while I took the life-guard test and went through the training. But then I drove home to bring the rest of my stuff back, and I can't really leave it all in a tent."

"I let him Z out on my floor last night," Justin explained.

The kitchen door swung open. Connor walked in, grumpy and rumpled. He nodded at Chelsea and gave a distasteful look at Alec's bare chest, a guarded glance at Justin, and a surprised look at Mooch. Then he put a battered teakettle on the stove.

"My stuff's on the top shelf in the yellow refrigerator," Justin said. "I moved it all onto one shelf, so we can keep it straight. And I stuck Mooch's food under the sink."

"Not a problem, right at the moment," Chelsea said. "I haven't exactly done my shopping yet."

"Do you fancy doughnuts?" Connor pointed with his chin to a large box at the end of the counter. "There's about three dozen in there."

Chelsea sighed with relief. "I told Kate you'd be good for *some*thing."

"I make doughnuts at O'Doul's O'Donuts," Connor explained to Justin and Alec. "Earning a princely sum, incidentally. I just got off shift at four thirty."

"Shouldn't you be sleeping?" Justin asked.

"I took a nap. And I like the morning for writing. I'll sleep some more in the afternoon."

Chelsea opened the box of doughnuts. Plain. Jelly. Honey glazed. Ah, chocolate frosted. That was the ticket for a good, healthy breakfast.

"Help yourselves," Connor said, waving to include Alec and Justin. "I hate the filthy things myself."

"Thanks." Alec lifted a jelly donut.

Justin finished his melon and tossed the rind into the trash. "Think I'll pass," he said, heading to the bathroom.

"So, what kind of stuff do you write?" Alec asked.

"Stuff that'll never be published," Connor said. "Poetry, mostly." He shrugged. "Some essays, some fiction."

"How is it an Irish guy ends up in O.C.?" Alec asked, "if you don't mind my asking?"

Connor studied the teapot. "Haven't you heard? This is the land of opportunity." The teapot whistled. "Tea all round?" he asked.

Alec shrugged. "I feel like a charity case."

"Yes or no?" Connor said.

"Yes," Chelsea said. Alec took a cup as well.

Kate walked in, looking fresh and confident and ready to conquer the world. Her sun-streaked hair was pulled back in a pretty French braid, and she was wearing a coral T-shirt that somehow managed to make her eyes look even bluer. "Morning, all," she said. Her eyes landed on Alec.

"You remember Alec," Chelsea said. "The guy from the Jeep on the bridge. It turns out he's a friend of Justin's."

"Small world," Kate said, shaking her head just as Mooch ran over to give her an exuberant welcome.

"He must know you," Alec said.

"So does his master," Connor commented wryly.

Kate shot Connor an annoyed look, but Chelsea distracted her with a jelly doughnut. "Look what Connor brought, Kate."

"Tea as well," Connor said. "If you'd care for some."

"Does it have caffeine?" Kate asked.

"It does, thank heavens."

"No thanks, then. They'll have decaf at work."

"Where's work?" Connor asked.

"The Safe Seas Foundation."

"Ah. Then I'm sure they'll have decaf," Connor remarked. "People in the business of saving the world insist on decaf. Herbal tea and all. Which may be one reason no one ever does quite get around to saving the planet."

"Kate doesn't need caffeine," Chelsea teased. "She's a sugar junkie. I once saw her eat an entire box of Twinkies during a rerun of *The Patty Duke Show*."

"But they're cousins, identical cousins—" Alec began to sing, but Connor's murderous glare cut him off cold.

"TV at its finest," Kate said. She took a bite of her donut. "Let me ask you this, Alec, since you're obviously a fan. Which cousin loses control when she sees a hot dog?"

Alec started to answer, but just then Grace wandered in and the room fell silent. She was wearing a blue silk bathrobe, and shielding her eyes from the sunlight streaming in the window. "For God's sake, someone pull the shade."

Not a morning person, Chelsea decided. "Doughnut?"

"I'd rather die a slow, lingering death." Grace searched the kitchen. "Doesn't anyone here drink coffee?"

"All we have is Connor's tea."

"Does it contain caffeine?"

Chelsea nodded.

"I'll have some, then, if you don't mind, Connor," Grace said. "I thought maybe it was one of those herbal concoctions. Grass clippings steeped in hot water."

Grace sipped her tea. "So. This is morning."

"I take it you like to sleep late?" Alec said. Were his eyes dwelling on the perilously open front of Grace's robe, or was that just Chelsea's imagination? No, he was definitely staring, watching the sliding fabric with a certain amused hopefulness.

"Normally I get up around noon. I work late. But this morning I could have sworn I heard someone singing the theme song from *The Brady Bunch*. I couldn't get back to sleep after that." Her gaze settled on Alec.

Alec blushed and suddenly became very interested in looking at the doughnut in his hand. "Um, I guess that was yours truly. You know how a tune will get stuck in your head. . . ."

Grace stared at him, bemused, making a point of looking him up and down. "Do you dance in the shower, too? I'm just trying to conjure up the right mental picture."

Alec blushed deeper. "No. I don't dance much. I mean, I know how and all, I just don't. I think I look like a dork when I dance. Especially dancing in the shower. Not that . . . not that I was."

Very interesting, Chelsea reflected. Grace had done that so smoothly. One minute Alec had been leering at her, and then, with just a few words and a look from those big almond eyes, she'd left Alec blushing and babbling like an idiot.

Grace craned her neck toward the bathroom door down the hall. "I need an aspirin. My head is killing me. Who's in the bathroom?"

"Justin," Chelsea said. "He's the guy who lives down in the boathouse."

"I know Justin."

"You *do*?" Chelsea sneaked a quick glance at Kate.

"We're both townies, remember?" Grace said. "In the off-season O.C.'s a pretty small place." She walked to the bathroom, opened the door, and stepped into a cloud of steam.

"She can't go in there," Kate objected.

"She just did," Chelsea said.

Alec shrugged and laughed. "That's Justin, for you. I worked with the dude yesterday, and I swear it's like he's this big babe magnet. Women are all over him."

Kate's eyes narrowed perceptibly. "It's late," she muttered. "I have to go to work." But she didn't move.

There was a male shout and a female laugh from the direction of the bathroom. Chelsea watched the color drain from Kate's face.

Finally Grace emerged, cradling two aspirins

in her palm. She retrieved her tea and downed the pills with a quick swallow.

"Bye," Kate said suddenly. "I don't want to be late."

"Hey, Kate, before you go—" Chelsea hesitated. "Our boy Alec here doesn't have a place to stay. And we still have one room open—"

"Fine, whatever you decide," Kate said, with a vague wave of her hand, her gaze still drawn toward the bathroom door where Justin was showering.

"Good luck," Chelsea said. "Knock those fishies dead."

Kate pulled her eyes from the door and smiled nervously. "See you tonight," she said, and she took off, her hiking boots echoing down the wood hallway.

"You sure this is okay?" Alec asked.

"Grace?" Chelsea asked.

Grace shrugged. "He has a good voice. Although if he wakes me up with it again, he'll be singing soprano."

"Connor?"

Connor shook his head doubtfully at Alec. "You will be wearing a shirt to meals at least, won't you?"

"There you go. You're in. As long as you have two hundred and seventy-five bucks." Chelsea held out her hand.

Alec was flattening out some wrinkled twenty-dollar bills when Justin came out of the shower. He was wearing a Red Cross T-shirt and his Beach Patrol shorts. "What did you do, rookie, con these girls into renting to you?"

"Looks that way," Alec said happily.

"He snores, so make sure he keeps his door closed at night," Justin warned. Then he shook his head in mock disapproval at Grace. "Flushing the toilet while I'm in the shower, Racey? Isn't that a little adolescent for you?"

"Hey, it's early and I haven't had any coffee."

Racey. *So,* Chelsea thought, *Justin knows Grace well enough to have a nickname for her.* Interesting.

Racey?

In the space of a second it all fell into place.

Racey was the name on the note Kate had found. Justin did know Grace well.

Very well.

TEN

"You. Give me a hand, will you? I need someone to hold Babycakes for me."

Kate stopped short in the tiny lobby of the Safe Seas Foundation. She stepped aside to make way for the vet or marine biologist or whoever it was the woman in the hallway was beckoning.

"Come on, come on," the woman said.

"Me?" Kate asked.

"Aren't you Katherine Quinn?"

"Call me Kate."

"Shelby Haynes." The woman extended a damp glove.

"You're Dr. Haynes?" Kate had expected the head honcho to be more scholarly looking, not this thirty-something redhead in a GREENPEACE T-shirt and cutoffs.

"Guilty. And by the way, it's Shelby. Only my

ex-husband has to call me Dr. Haynes." She was already halfway down the hall, her bare feet slapping on the tile floor. "Come on. I need a hand."

Kate trotted after her. She followed Shelby to a cluttered, brightly lit lab. The marine biologist was leaning over a narrow glass tank that was an offshoot of a much larger tank. Inside, barely able to move in the narrow confines, was a four-foot-long shark.

"Here." Shelby tossed Kate a pair of the same heavy gloves she was wearing. "They won't help if you stick your finger in his mouth, but they're good for morale."

Kate gulped. "That's a shark."

"It's a lemon shark," Shelby corrected. "His name's Babycakes." She reached in and stroked the long gunmetal-gray back of the shark. "I have to give him a shot. Friday is shot day for Babycakes."

Slowly Kate approached the shark and pulled on the gloves. "What's wrong with him?" she managed to ask.

"Wrong? Nothing, unfortunately." Shelby took off her gloves and began filling a large syringe from a vial. "We're trying like hell to give him cancer."

"You're trying to *give* him cancer?" Kate drew back unconsciously.

Shelby nodded as she cleared the syringe of air. "Yes. You see, sharks almost never get cancer. We think that fact might be helpful someday in developing cancer-fighting drugs for humans. We've pumped Babycakes full of enough toxins and carcinogens to grow a tumor the size of the Astrodome, and he refuses to get sick."

Kate stared into the tank. They were trying to give a shark cancer? She thought this place was called the *Safe* Seas Foundation.

"Look, I'm sorry for throwing you to the wolves like this."

"The sharks, you mean."

Shelby laughed. "I remember from your application you'd been hoping to work on the whale-monitoring program."

Kate nodded. She'd gone on a whale-watch tour last summer with Justin, and ever since, she'd been hooked. "They're so . . . amazing," she said.

"I went through my whale phase in grad school. Then I saw my first shark up close and it was love at first bite." Shelby stroked Babycakes again. "So perfectly evolved. So . . . beautiful. They've been around for hundreds of millions of years."

"So have roaches." Kate checked the hall. Where were the other employees? The *sane* employees?

Shelby grinned. "I'll make a believer of you yet."

Kate approached the tank timidly. Her hand would just fit inside Babycakes's jaws. "He's had breakfast, right?"

"That wouldn't help. Sharks pretty much stay hungry. Now, all I want you to do is grab him at the tail and midway down his back to hold him steady. I doubt he'll move. He's used to the routine."

"You *doubt* he'll move?"

"Hey, Shel. Trouble with Babycakes?" A guy about Kate's age came into the room.

"Kate Quinn, meet Andrew McKittrick," Shelby said. "He interned here last summer, and I'm sure he'll be happy to show you the ropes."

Kate yanked her eyes away from Babycakes. Andrew was a definite improvement. He had a nice, strong jaw. Kate liked that in a guy. And a nice, wide smile. She liked that, too. Not to mention the wavy blond hair and the very blue eyes. Kate guessed that Andrew was a year or two older than she; he had that confident college-guy grin. Like Shelby, he was dressed in cutoffs and a faded T-shirt. Unlike Shelby, he was definitely taking a long look at her legs.

Andrew extended his hand. "Welcome aboard," he said.

Kate couldn't help gasping. Two of the fingers on his right hand were missing.

"It's nothing," Andrew said. He slipped his hand into his jeans pocket. "I was helping Shelby out last summer with a hammerhead shark, and, well . . ."

Kate watched in horror as he gave a little wave and disappeared down the hallway.

"Don't mind Andrew," Shelby said dismissively. "He tries that on all the interns."

"Tries?" Kate repeated.

Shelby paused, her syringe in midair. "Relax, Kate," she said. "All of us here can still count to ten on our fingers. Now grab on."

Next time she interned, she'd be sure to read the application a little more carefully. With a deep breath Kate eased her gloved hands into the tank, barely making a ripple. Babycakes rolled slightly, turning his menacing, unblinking stare on her.

"Good," Shelby said. "I think he likes you."

Kate managed a nervous smile and wondered if it was too late to get a job making taffy or funnel cakes.

Shelby jabbed the needle into Babycakes's gray flesh. "He didn't even move," Kate whispered.

"How's it going?" asked Andrew, passing by

113

with an armful of manila files.

"I told Kate about the fingers, Andrew."

"I couldn't resist," Andrew said, hopping onto a counter. "So you're all settled in O.C.?" he asked.

"Yes," Kate answered distractedly. Then she remembered the scene at the house that morning—the house that she was desperately trying to move out of. "Um, well, in a way, no," she amended. "I mean, I'm temporarily settled."

"What, you don't like the palatial dwelling we arranged for you?" Shelby demanded.

"Actually, I'm staying somewhere else. It's a long story. But now I'm just having some housing difficulties."

"Difficulties with the house," Shelby asked as she wrote something on a chart, "or difficulties with the residents of the house?"

"That's an even longer story, but it's the latter, I guess you'd say." It was all so complicated. Besides, she didn't want to sound like a flake on her first hour at work. She should at least give it a day or two. "It's not that all my roommates aren't perfectly nice," she tried to explain, "it's just that I, uh, can't live with them."

Both Shelby and Andrew laughed. "That's why I live alone at college," he said.

"Where do you go to school?" The shark

squirmed slightly and Kate gulped. There was no way Babycakes could turn around and get her unless he did a full somersault. Did sharks do somersaults?

"Harvard." Andrew gave a self-deprecating laugh. "But don't hold it against me."

"Are you kidding?" Kate said. "I'm really impressed. What are you studying?"

"Biochem. I want to do cancer research eventually. That's why I'm here at Safe Seas for another summer. Shelby's shark research is really cutting edge—although she's far too modest to admit it. When she wins the Nobel someday, I want to be there to hear her thank all the little people who helped make it possible."

Shelby grinned and nodded toward the hallway. "I think I hear the phone, little person. Wanna grab it?"

"Sure." Andrew gave Kate another smile. "Meet me in the office when you're done here and we'll do the grand-tour thing, okay?"

Kate nodded, her eyes still riveted on the strange creature in her grasp.

"Kate?" Shelby said. "You can let go now."

"Oh." Kate released Babycakes and drew her hands from the water. "Sorry. It was just so . . . so weird, touching something everyone's afraid of, you know?" She peered into the tank.

"They really are beautiful, aren't they?"

Shelby nodded. "It's the dangerous things in life that are often most seductive," she said in a serious, thoughtful voice. Then she laughed. "Hey, I better write that down. It'll be great in my Nobel acceptance speech."

Grace settled the little cooler on the sand and spread her beach towel out, using mounds of sand to hold the corners down. The sun, undiminished by even the hint of a cloud, had raised the temperature of the sand to frying-pan heat. Fortunately an intermittent breeze was blowing salty and cool.

She kicked her sandals aside and pulled off her shorts. She had on a blue man's work shirt, tied in front, open most of the way. She untied the knot and piled the shirt with her shoes and shorts. The two-piece bathing suit underneath was the same deep green as her eyes and so sheer that it clung to her like a second skin.

She sat down and pulled a can of beer from the cooler, slipping it into a foam holder that hid the label. After a quick preliminary sip, she stretched her long legs, digging her toes into the cooler sand beneath the surface. Then she began slathering on baby oil, working methodically from ankle to thigh. So what if baby oil had an SPF of zero? Screw skin cancer. And screw that holier-than-thou voice in her own head that told her drinking a beer before noon was a sign that something wasn't quite right in Graceland.

She took a longer, more satisfying swig. Alcohol was a big no-no on the beach, but who was going to bust her? The Beach Patrol?

She scanned the beach. Justin was in his chair, maybe fifty feet away. "Here's to you, babe," she said.

She rolled over and waited for the beer to hit and the worry to fade. She'd finally gotten hold of Bo this morning. She'd tried to call him from The Claw last night, but her mother had answered every time. And every time, Grace had hung up. Not very adult. But arguing with her mom was a long trip to nowhere. This morning she'd given Bo her address, made him promise to call her if he needed anything. He'd sounded cool, said he had big plans for the summer, but there was something about his voice that had left her feeling wired and anxious. And very guilty.

She glanced down the beach toward Justin and wondered if he'd noticed her yet. She also wondered if there was some deep psychological reason why she'd just happened to end up on his particular turf. Coincidence, she told herself, nothing more. Just like it was coincidence she'd happened to end up living at his particular address. Ocean City was a small town, after all, in some ways. Too small.

In any case, she was glad there was a familiar face at the house. Through most of high school they'd had an on-again, off-again thing—more off than on, actually. But they'd always stayed friends, and that had meant a lot, especially since she and Justin had remained on the social fringes by choice. She'd really missed Justin when he'd decided to quit school.

It hadn't surprised her when he'd quit, though. Justin was your classic loner. So was she, when you got right down to it. She could party hard and play the social games, but for the most part she kept her distance from people. Of course, she'd never had any problem getting dates, when she wanted them. Guys weren't a problem. Girls, on the other hand, never seemed to like her much. Justin said it was because she intimidated them.

Well, screw them, too. She took another drink and rolled over. For a moment she wondered what her new roommates, the two girls, thought of her. Chelsea seemed forever to be watching her, not intrusively, just with curiosity. Chelsea had told her she was an artist;

maybe she was that way with everyone.

As for Kate, she seemed nice enough. But there was something about that girl . . . Grace couldn't quite put her finger on it, but she had the feeling she and Kate weren't going to hit it off. Maybe it was just that fresh, athletic, sun-streaked blond thing. She'd known girls like Kate in high school—bursting with good health and cheerfulness, every guy's best friend, every girl's best friend. Golden Girls.

Grace closed her eyes behind her sunglasses. The sun was nothing but a red glow through her eyelids. The heat felt wonderful on her skin, but the brightness, that relentless blinding light . . . Maybe that was it. Maybe it was that Kate seemed like such a creature of daylight and clear blue skies. Grace much preferred the cooler, subtler, more secretive world that appeared after the sun went down.

As for the rest of the crew, well, they seemed okay enough. Alec was good-looking, although he had a little bit of that prom-king perfection, the kind of guy who could get by on a flash of his smile. Connor she wasn't so sure about. He got an A on the sense-of-humor scale, but she had the feeling there was more to him than he was letting on. Of course, that was true of her, too. Maybe it was true of everybody.

Another drink. Already the beer was getting warm. Connor would probably approve. Wasn't that how the Irish drank it?

After a while Grace dozed off. She hadn't been asleep long when she awoke with a start. She'd been having a dream—a very sexy dream—about Justin. They were on his boat, all alone at sea, and the sun was beating down, and she'd been in his arms . . . She shook away the details. Dreams. They were stray neuron impulses, nothing more.

She stashed the beer back in her cooler and stood. Justin could probably use some company. The sand was sizzling. She should have slipped on her sandals. "What a cushy gig," she called when she was close enough to be heard over the surf.

Justin turned. His mirrored shades kept her from tracking his eyes, but she could tell by the way his head dropped that he was checking her out. As if there were any surprises left.

She returned the favor, letting her gaze skate over his form. He looked even better than he had last summer—leaner and more muscular. She'd forgotten how broad his shoulders were.

Grace leaned against his chair. "I run my butt off at The Claw for a few lousy bucks, and you sit here all day and gawk at the bikinis."

"All in the line of duty." Justin returned his eyes to the water. Nothing personal, she knew, just regulations. Lifeguards were supposed to keep their eyes on the water at all times.

"What brings you down this way?" he asked.

"Oh, I don't know." Grace sighed. "It's my day off, and I thought I'd see if my suit still fit."

"It fits."

She liked the way he said it. "I just had a dream about you," she admitted.

"Dream, as in nightmare?"

She laughed. "That depends. We were in your boat."

"Now that's a *good* dream."

"Out in the middle of the ocean."

"A *very* good dream."

"And we weren't wearing any clothes."

No answer, just that slow smile.

Grace smiled back. "Don't you think it's weird, our living together? I mean, back in high school, when we were an item, I used to have fantasies about what it would be like. And now . . ." Her voice trailed off.

"And now," Justin continued, "here we are, flushing and showering together in domestic bliss."

"Did you tell anyone about us?" Grace asked suddenly.

"It's none of their business. You?"

Grace shook her head. "Nope. Besides, I've hardly spoken to most of them. What do you think of everybody?"

Justin shrugged.

"They're okay, I guess," she continued. "Alec and Connor seem mellow. So does Chelsea. Kate"—she paused—"I'm not so sure about yet."

Justin kept his eyes on the ocean. "Why's that?"

"I don't know. Not my type, I guess."

He smiled, a grim, faraway sort of smile.

Grace stared up at him quizzically. Suddenly Justin popped his whistle in his mouth and stood. He gave a couple shrill blows and waved some kids in inner tubes closer to shore. The kids swam in obediently. "I was kind of surprised you moved out of your mom's place," Justin said as he sat down. He paused. "How's Ellen doing, anyway?"

"Bad. Really bad. That's why I had to get out. And her boyfriend was putting the moves on me—" Grace's voice broke.

Justin kept his eyes on the water. "I'm sorry, Racey," he said softly. "It's good you're out of there."

Grace let her head fall against his leg. It was hot and hard and felt good against her cheek. "I feel so bad," she whispered. "About Bo. Maybe I should have stayed."

"He'll be okay. Bo's a tough kid."

"Not so tough. Not always."

Justin stroked her hair. "What about your dad?"

"He sends money. Not that she needs it. But he's out in California, Justin. He and his new wife just had their second kid. There's no room for Bo in his life, and Bo senses it."

"We'll keep an eye on him, you and me."

Grace pulled herself together and forced a smile. "I could've picked a worse housemate than you, I guess."

Justin let his arm drop. "Whatever you do, don't go back, Racey. You did the right thing."

"I hope you're right."

"I am," Justin said. He paused. "Sometimes," he said slowly, "you just have to let things go."

ELEVEN

"So, Chelsea, I see from your application that you've never waited tables before."

"No, ma'am, I haven't."

"If you were serving a fried seafood platter of shrimp, fish, and scallops, would you include tartar sauce or cocktail sauce?"

"Um, tartar sauce?"

"No."

"Cocktail sauce! That's what I meant to say."

"Actually, you would include both. It's a trick question."

"Oh. Well, I could learn."

"Sorry, but I have plenty of applicants who wouldn't need to be trained."

"Chelsea. That's a nice name."

"Thanks."

"Chelsea, let me ask you something. Where do you see yourself five years from now?"

"Excuse me?"

"I mean, do you see yourself as having a future in bathing-apparel sales?"

"I never really thought about it."

"It's a growth industry. There's tons of potential. Look at me. Three years ago I was a bouncer at a strip joint. Now I own the hottest bathing-apparel store in Ocean City."

"That's great."

"I drive a Corvette. Next year I'm getting a Viper. Four hundred horsepower, you know. Fastest thing on the road."

"So can I have the job?"

"Well, you'd have to wear our line. I like my girls to show off what we sell. How do you look in a bikini?"

"Okay, I guess."

"Would you mind trying one on?"

"I guess not. Where's the dressing room?"

"Oh, don't go all shy on me. You can change right here. We're all friends here. I like to stay close to my girls. Hey! Hey, wait! There's a lot of potential . . ."

"What can I do for you?"

"I'm looking for a job."

"A job? Doing what? This is a machine shop."

"I could answer phones."

"What phones? Can you operate a drill press?"

"A what?"

"A what, she asks me. A drill press."

"Well—"

"How about a lathe?"

"Hmm. No restaurant experience."

"No, but I'm really eager to learn."

"That just shows how inexperienced you are. No one in his right mind wants to wait tables. So let me ask you. Say you've got an order for a fried seafood platter. What do you give the people, tartar sauce or cocktail sauce?"

"Both."

"Both? Are you nuts? So they can just throw it away? You ask the people which one they want. Both! Like I'm made out of money."

"You're welcome to fill out an application."

"Do you have any jobs?"

"No, not right now."

"Then why should I fill out an application?"

"We may have job openings later in the season. We'll keep your application on file."

"And then you call the people who put in applications?"

126

"Yes, that's the procedure."

"Let me ask you something. How many applications do you already have on file?"

"About two hundred, I believe."

Chelsea stuck a straw into her lemonade and took a deep swallow. She'd walked half the two-mile length of the boardwalk and spoken to what seemed like hundreds of people. It was late afternoon, and so far she hadn't gotten so much as a nibble.

This sucked. She should be lying out there on that beautiful beach, not walking up and down these boards in her Responsible Outfit—sweaty dress, sweatier panty hose, excruciating shoes. She should be checking out the volleyball players and the cute lifeguards. . . .

Speaking of which.

She wondered if Justin and Alec were working around this area. The lifeguard chairs were too far down toward the water for her to get a good look at their occupants. Of course, from what Alec had said, Justin's chair should be easy to find. All she had to do was look for the groupies circling it like vultures.

Quite possibly one of those girls could be Grace. Not that Grace struck her as the groupie type, of course. Grace was way too cool, way too sophisticated, for that. As a matter of fact, from what she'd seen so far, Chelsea was really impressed with Grace. Unfortunately, there was no way they could be friends, not if Grace was the one who'd broken up Justin and Kate. After all, Kate was Chelsea's best friend in the world.

And best friends always told each other everything.

Or did they? If she told Kate about Grace, Kate would refuse to spend another night in the house. Which would be a shame; the house was great. And they'd put together a pretty interesting bunch of roommates.

Like Connor, for instance. Chelsea wouldn't mind getting to know him a little better. He was different from the guys she'd known in high school, and it wasn't just because of that great Irish accent. Maybe it was because he wasn't afraid to talk openly about wanting to be a writer. She wished she had the nerve to be the same way about her art, but she'd heard way too many jokes from her family about starving artists for that.

Chelsea rattled the ice in her cup, then tossed it into one of the blue steel drums that lined the boardwalk and the beach.

So what should she do about the Justin-Grace situation? Maybe the real question was, what was best for Kate? Well, that was obvious. She needed to stay in the house and deal with her feelings for Justin. And Kate would be miserable if she knew the truth about Grace. It was Chelsea's job to protect her best friend's interests.

Job. That ugly word again. "Okay," she muttered. "Another half hour of job hunting, then I admit defeat."

Of course, if she didn't get a job, Greg would never let her live it down. He couldn't understand why she wanted to spend their last summer before college apart, working at some menial job far away from him. The truth was, she wasn't exactly sure either. But something told her it was a good idea to be on her own for a little while. What was three months, in the grand scheme of things? And the truth was, she was kind of enjoying this time away from him. They'd been dating for nearly six months, a real Olympic record for Chelsea.

She gazed off down the boardwalk. Next up was a fast-food place specializing in Mexican food. *"Tina Wina Taco,"* she said under her breath. "I wonder if I should include salsa or hot sauce or both."

She took a deep breath and approached the girl behind the counter. "Would you like to try our three-taco special?" the girl asked.

"Actually, I'm looking for a job," Chelsea said.

"Me too."

Chelsea glanced behind her. The voice belonged to a cute boy, maybe fourteen or fifteen, with a skateboard in one hand. A lock of dark hair hung low over one eye. His black T-shirt was ripped to stylish shreds.

"I asked first," Chelsea growled.

"Hey, don't pop a vein, all right?" the boy said.

Chelsea sighed. "Sorry. It's been a long day."

"You want to fill out an application?" the girl asked.

"Do I have a choice?" Chelsea took the clipboard with the application. "My friend here wants to apply too."

"How old are you, kid?"

"I'm fifteen, all right?"

"Sorry, dude. You have to be sixteen."

"Okay, so I'm sixteen. I forgot. I had a birthday."

Chelsea felt sorry for the kid. He looked strangely desperate and, despite the tough act, vulnerable. But her pity was short-lived. When the counter girl refused to give him an application, the kid cut loose a torrent of obscene abuse aimed at the girl, Mexican food in general, and life as a whole. Then he hopped on his board and sped away.

"Friend of yours?" the manager asked Chelsea, arriving just in time to catch the last few insults.

"No," Chelsea said as she watched him ride away. "Just another job hunter."

"This sauce is great. Old family recipe?" Alec asked that evening as he twirled his spaghetti around his fork. He elbowed Justin, who was sitting beside him at the huge wooden table in the dining room.

"Oh, yeah," Justin said quickly. "It's great."

"It's Ragu," Chelsea admitted. "Chunky Garden Style with Mushrooms. But I added the meatballs myself."

"Don't apologize, Chelsea," Kate said. "It's how my mom makes spaghetti too. Although she uses linguini."

"Ah, linguini," Connor said. "A pasta similar to spaghetti, only flatter. Flatter and wider still, you're talking fettucini. Then, on the other end of the spectrum, you have your spaghettini, or thin spaghetti, and angelhair, thinner still."

Everyone at the table turned to stare at Connor, who shrugged. "In this day and age, when so few women know how to cook, it's a good idea for a fellow to learn the basics."

This was good, Chelsea decided. So far everyone seemed to be having a fine time. Just as she'd hoped, having a big dinner together was giving everyone a chance to get to know each other. Sort of a Unity Dinner. Maybe they'd all become one big happy family, and Kate would realize there was no need to move out. Maybe Kate and Grace would even manage to bond. After all, they had a lot in common. Like Justin, for example.

On the other hand, if Justin happened to open his mouth and call Grace *Racey*, well . . . she had deliberately avoided putting any knives on the table.

Kate reached for another roll. "I can't believe how hungry I am," she said. "I was so nervous about work this morning, I forgot to bring any lunch. If Andrew hadn't given me half his sandwich, I'd have passed out by now."

"Andrew?" Chelsea asked.

"An intern at Safe Seas."

"A cute intern?" Chelsea pressed.

"Very cute, actually," Kate said. "He's from Maine. He just finished his first year at Harvard."

Chelsea sneaked a glance at Justin to check out his reaction to Andrew from Maine. Nothing. He was letting Mooch lick his plate clean.

"Anyone want a beer?" Grace asked.

"That'd be lovely," Connor said casually.

But Chelsea felt herself tense up. Beer? "Grace, are you twenty-one? I thought you said you were only eighteen."

Grace waved her hand airily. "Age is just a state of mind."

"I don't drink," Alec said.

"It's only weak American beer," Connor said. "The stuff is practically water."

Alec shook his head doubtfully. "You know, it *is* illegal in this country. The drinking age is twenty-one."

"Let me guess," Grace said, giving Alec a mocking look. "Your body is a temple, right?"

Alec blushed. "I have a swim scholarship to college, and I just try to take care of myself. Keep myself in shape—"

"That doesn't appear to be a problem," Grace said.

Kate cleared her throat. "If Chelsea and Alec are uncomfortable about having alcohol in the house, maybe we should talk about it," she said. "I'm not necessarily thrilled about it either. Like Alec said, there is this annoying little law."

The silence that followed was deafening.

Without a word Grace got up, walked from the dining room into the kitchen, and came back a moment later with two bottles of beer. She set one in front of Connor. Then she took a swig from the other and sat down, looking defiantly at the others.

"Look, it's just that we haven't decided as a group what the house policy should be," Kate said. "I'm open-minded on the question myself, as long as no one's drinking and driving or flying a 747. But I don't want to put anyone in a position where they feel like they're breaking a law."

"Simple enough," Grace said. "We'll do it democratically. All in favor of letting people decide for themselves whether to bring alcohol into the house, raise your hands."

Grace and Connor both raised their hands.

"I don't think I should get a vote," Justin said. "I live in the boathouse. What I do there's my business."

"Two out of five," Alec pointed out. "That's not a majority."

Chelsea took a deep breath. "Actually, I guess I don't want to vote against it either. I mean, this is our first home *without* parents around to dictate rules." She looked over at Kate. "And you know me—I've only had like three beers in my whole life—but I think we should try to be laid back about rules, so I don't really want to tell other people . . ."

Chelsea's voice trailed off. The truth was, she agreed with Alec, but she absolutely hated confrontations of any kind. She just didn't feel like this was something they should start a big fight over, especially when everybody was starting to get along. She felt a little stab of guilt. Okay, so she was spineless. So what? It made life easier in the long run.

"I'll vote with Alec," Kate said, sending him a smile.

Alec shook his head. "Look, it's no biggie. Grace and Connor can drink, as far as I'm concerned. I was just saying . . . never mind." He looked down at his plate, clearly uncomfortable. "I thought we should discuss it. Now we have. Majority rules."

"It's decided," Grace announced, clinking her bottle with Connor's. She turned her gaze first on Alec, then Chelsea, then settled on Kate. "So, is there anything else you don't want me doing? Staying up late? Hanging out with the wrong crowd? Watching MTV? Or, say"—she executed a perfect dramatic pause—"having sex?"

Suddenly the Unity Dinner looked as if it was about to get nasty. "I'm for everyone making their own decisions about what they do in their own bedrooms," Chelsea interjected quickly. "Common areas, like the kitchen, living room, and dining room, we'll vote on, if there are disagreements."

"That sounds like a good idea," Kate said smoothly. "Which I suppose just means that Grace will need a majority vote before she can have sex on the dining-room table."

"Point goes to Kate," Connor said. "I think that makes it two to one, Grace's favor."

"How about if we call it a draw?" Justin suggested with a sidelong glance at Connor.

For a while everyone ate in tense silence. It was a good thing, Chelsea decided, that she hadn't yet told her friend about Justin and Grace. After all, a fair amount of damage could be inflicted with a fork.

"I got a job today," Chelsea announced to no one in particular. "Actually, a job and a half, sort of."

Kate looked up from her plate. "That's great, Chelsea," she said brightly. "What kind of job is it?"

Chelsea shrugged. "The half a job is for the guy who runs the Best Body on the Beach contest. It's just for a few hours a week, really. Organizing his paperwork."

Grace made a face. "Best Body on the Beach? That meat parade?"

"I'm not thrilled about that aspect of it either," Chelsea admitted. "But I didn't feel I could turn anything down. Besides, like I said, it's only for a couple of hours."

"It's just good, clean fun," Justin said.

"It's a bunch of women wiggling their butt-cheeks," Kate said, rolling her eyes.

Great, Chelsea thought. At least there was one point of agreement between Grace and Kate.

"Wiggling butt-cheeks, you say?" Connor said, suddenly alert. "Should you need any help in . . . handling . . . the contestants, don't hesitate to call on me."

"What was the other job, Chelsea?" Alec asked.

"Believe it or not, it's an even dumber job. Although it isn't sexist, at least. It's for Tina Wina Taco. A Mexican place on the boardwalk."

"You're going to be making tacos?" Kate asked.

"No, I'm going to *be* a taco. See, they have a costume, this giant taco with a frilly Mexican skirt around the bottom. It's Tina Taco, their mascot. Well, I'm supposed to wear the costume and give out coupons to people. You're looking at the new Tina Taco." She made a wry face. "I see it as a piece of performance art—kind of Dada, not that anyone but me knows or cares what that means. Also, it pays a little over minimum wage."

Chelsea's announcement was met with silence. Several of her housemates seemed to be biting their lips. Alec was the first to put a hand over his mouth to stifle a laugh.

"Chelsea?" Connor asked. "Will you be terribly offended if we all just go ahead and laugh and get it out of our systems?"

Which was the point when Alec lost it, followed by everyone else in the room.

Finally, Chelsea thought with relief. Unity achieved.

TWELVE

"Is there some reason you're staring blankly at a bowl of leftover meatballs?" Chelsea asked when she walked into the kitchen later that evening.

Kate looked up. "I'm thinking about feeding these to Mooch. I can't throw food away. On the other hand, I really don't want to have to eat them either."

Chelsea pulled a soda out of the fridge. "Thanks. We'll just see how good *you* are at cooking."

"Why don't you take these down to Mooch?" Kate suggested casually. "It's a shame to let them go to waste."

"It was your idea. *You* take them down to Mooch."

"I can't. I'm busy wiping this counter."

"He won't bite, you know."

Kate cocked an eye at Chelsea. "Which one?"

"Look." Chelsea gulped her soda. "I'm in the middle of a chess game with Connor."

"You don't play chess."

"He's teaching me how. And when I'm done losing to him, I've got to go call my parents and tell them I'm not dead yet, and that's about all the fun and games I can stand for one night."

Kate stared at the bowl. Leftovers really weren't good for dogs anyway. Kibble. That was the ticket.

Alec poked his head in the kitchen. "Justin still here?"

"He's down at the boathouse," Chelsea answered.

"Well, our boss just called. He wants Justin to cover a shift tomorrow."

"Our first official phone call," Chelsea exclaimed. "Kate will tell him, Alec. She was just heading down there."

"Chels!" Kate cried, but Alec had already vanished.

"Later." Chelsea headed for the door. "I've got to get back to my game. Even if you and Justin are finished, you can still have joint custody of the dog, you know."

Kate stared at the cold meatballs. They'd probably just give Mooch indigestion. They'd given her a major case.

She picked up the bowl and headed toward the porch. Chelsea and Connor were playing chess in the living room. Alec was zoning out on the couch while an episode of *Love Connection* blared on the TV. Grace had gone out for the evening. Maybe that was why the house seemed so calm.

Kate closed the door to the porch behind her. The night was cool. The water lapped soothingly against the moorings of the boathouse. Several frogs were carrying on a heated debate on the lawn.

Through the porch screen Kate could just make out Mooch's shadowy form on the dock. He was watching something in the water. From a distance he really did remind her a lot of her own dog.

Something that felt suspiciously like homesickness washed over her. Impossible. How could she be homesick? She'd just gotten here. Well, maybe it wasn't homesickness, exactly. She just felt overwhelmed. And why shouldn't she? She was living in a house she couldn't afford. Her ex-boyfriend was living with her. And she'd spent her first day on the job trying to give cancer to a shark.

She eased open the porch door and stepped onto the lawn. A soft yellow light shone in the boathouse window. "Mooch," she whispered. "Come here, baby."

Mooch turned around and thumped his tail on the dock.

"Here, Mooch."

He rolled onto his back, beckoning her with soulful brown eyes that caught the moonlight. It figured. He never *had* obeyed well. Her own dog could do all kinds of tricks, everything short of bringing her breakfast in bed. Still, Mooch was a good old guy. A little learning-disabled, maybe, but he tried hard, and he caught a mean Frisbee.

She crossed the grass, cool and damp beneath her bare feet, then left wet footprints on the old wooden slats of the pier. "Look, Mooch," she whispered, setting down the bowl. Mooch leaped into action, burying his muzzle in the bowl. After the first two meatballs, he paused just long enough to slobber affectionately on her hand.

The bay water lapped against the pilings, sometimes softly, sometimes insistently. Kate bent over and traced a line through the smooth black surface, rinsing her hand clean. The water was wonderfully warm to the touch, almost body temperature. Perhaps later she could go for another swim.

Behind her, the side door to the boathouse

creaked open, framing Justin in a rectangle of light. "I see he's living up to his name," Justin remarked. He was wearing a pair of threadbare cutoffs and a faded blue T-shirt. QUESTION AUTHORITY, it read. She'd given him the shirt last summer.

"I'm surprised you still have that thing," she said.

"I like the sentiment." He closed the door.

They fell silent for a moment, listening to Mooch suck down the last of the meatballs. Kate waited for the awful awkwardness to start, or the angry recriminations, but she felt oddly calm. Maybe it was the darkness. It was like wearing a mask. She didn't feel as vulnerable.

"That was some dinner," Justin finally said.

Kate nodded. "Don't tell Chels, but I took a double dose of Alka-Seltzer."

"I meant the conversation, not the food," Justin said. "But they were both a little rough." He glanced back toward the house. "Don't let Grace get to you. She's . . ." He shrugged. "Complicated."

"She didn't bother me," Kate replied. She paused. *Complicated?* "You know Grace pretty well, then?" she asked, trying to sound casual.

"Well enough. She's not as tough as she seems."

Kate reached down to stroke Mooch's ears. So

Justin knew Grace well. So they were old friends. Why should that matter to Kate?

"I hope you don't mind my feeding Mooch," she said at last, forcing her thoughts away from Grace. "Our vet says leftovers are really bad for Oberon."

"The world's most pretentious dog name."

"Well, it lacks the class of *Mooch,* I admit." Kate tilted her chin. "There's nothing wrong with naming your dog after a character in Shakespeare. Oberon was—"

"I know who Oberon was," Justin said, his voice taking on a barely perceptible edge. "The king of the fairies in *A Midsummer Night's Dream.* Like I said, pretentious. Still," he continued, his voice relaxing, "Mooch and he were buddies last summer. Remember that time we went on a picnic and they decided to roll in some dead fish on the beach?"

Kate laughed. "They stank for a week."

"You had some good dog times together, huh, Mooch?" Justin said.

The conversation drifted away. "Well," Kate said, reaching down for the empty bowl, "I should get going."

Justin hooked his thumbs in his pockets and shrugged. "Thanks for the leftovers."

"Oh. I almost forgot. Alec said your boss

called. He wants you to pick up a shift tomorrow."

"Damn." Justin scowled. "I hate working Saturdays. Besides, I wanted to get some work done on my boat."

"You mean it's still floating?"

"O ye of little faith." Justin crossed his arms over his chest and gave Kate a look of supreme disappointment. "She's not just floating, she's practically ready to fly. Want to take a look?"

"No," Kate said automatically. She was in no mood to revisit the scene of Justin's crime.

"Come on. I don't have all that many people to show off to."

Don't you? she wondered. But when he took her arm, she relented.

Inside the boathouse was cool and dark. It was built on pylons that kept the floor level just two feet above the lapping water at high tide. The twenty-eight-foot sailboat, its mast removed, was nestled into a narrow berth, with a huge, barnlike door behind it. With the door open, the boat could easily be launched out onto the open water. On the landward side, a narrow staircase led up to a loft. Kate could see Justin's bed, pushed right up next to the loft railing so it overlooked the boat.

"Must get humid in here," she observed.

"Windy, too. These walls are full of chinks and holes, not to mention what blows in under the gate. And in the winter, forget it."

"You actually stayed here last winter?"

"Yeah, like an idiot." He laughed softly. "The price was right."

"I figured you'd moved with your mom to Vermont."

"She's got her own life now. I didn't want to cramp her style."

Kate gazed at the workbench set up beneath the overhang of the loft. A circular saw lay there, along with various boards and mounds of sawdust. "Well," she said, "I'll say one thing. This definitely has character."

"The marina closes down over the winter. I found this place so I could work on it anytime I was in the mood. Come on, take a look inside."

"I've seen the inside."

Justin smiled. It was still a great smile, even if she no longer cared. "Come on, take a look. I love to show off my work, and it's changed since you saw it last."

I saw it last when I found that note, Kate thought. But she took his hand. It was stronger and more callused than she remembered. He'd been working hard. She followed Justin down three steps, ducking her head to get into the

146

cabin. It was pitch-black, and Kate felt him reach for the light, brushing his arm across her chest.

An accident? Probably. Still, it gave Kate an odd, electric feeling—half memory, half anticipation. A sudden image from last summer flashed through her mind, of the two of them sitting late at night in his lifeguard stand on an abandoned beach. No moon to fade the piercing lights of the stars overhead. A chill breeze that made them bundle close together. He had kissed her and turned the night warm. She had shivered as he unzipped her sweatshirt and slipped his roughened hand beneath her shirt.

Kate took a step forward while Justin fumbled for the light, and this time it was her hand that grazed his arm. Justin caught her hand in his. Kate stopped breathing. She could sense him there, invisible, only inches away. They were moving closer. Their bodies touched, her leg against his, the tender inside of her wrist brushing against the sandpaper of his jaw, her cheek buried on his hard warm chest.

Their lips came together perfectly, though neither could see, and Kate felt a sweet heat surge through her body. Justin pulled away gently, then returned for more kisses, letting them rain lightly on her cheeks, her forehead, the sensitive hollow of her neck.

She was melting in sensation, losing herself to him, only, some tiny, rational part of herself knew it was all wrong. Suddenly she pulled away. Or had it been Justin who pulled back?

She couldn't be sure. But when the light snapped on, his face was impassive. *Forget it,* his dark eyes said, *it never happened.* It had never happened. It could never happen. They'd tried this before, and it hadn't worked.

Justin turned away from her. "See?" he said huskily. "I'm about halfway done with the galley—the kitchen. Two-burner gimballed stove—gimballed," he explained, "means it can stay level when the boat rocks. Microwave oven, built-in coffee maker."

"No dishwasher, huh?" She was proud of the way her voice stayed even.

"Everything but. Here, watch your head and I'll show you the master cabin." He led the way through the galley, past the minuscule bathroom, and into the low-ceilinged bedroom in the front of the boat.

"Built-in stereo speakers." He pointed to two round speakers set neatly into the teak paneling.

Kate noticed a small bookshelf crammed with books. Most were on boatbuilding and navigation. But she also noticed a worn copy of *The Sound and the Fury*.

"You're reading Faulkner?" she asked.

Justin shrugged. "You said you liked him, so I thought . . . what the hell."

"Did you enjoy it?"

"Not a whole lot," he admitted. "Sorry. I guess maybe it's a little over my head."

He seemed embarrassed, and Kate was instantly sorry she'd brought it up. She reached for one of the navigation books and opened it. The page was covered with diagrams and equations. "But *this* isn't over your head?" she asked.

"Hey, trigonometry is over everyone's head. But you have to know it if you're going to navigate."

"And you can do that, but you can't get through some Faulkner?"

"I can learn what I need to learn," Justin said coolly. "I taught myself cabinetry and wiring and a lot of other things because I needed to know them for what I want to do. I guess I don't figure I'll need much American lit. when I'm sailing."

"But if you went to college, you could learn all those things and more. You're one of the smartest people I know, Justin. You could really *do* something with your life."

Justin took a step back. Yes, Kate realized, she had reopened part of the argument that had driven them apart. It was too late to take back the words now, and besides, they were true.

"Nothing's changed, has it, Kate?" Justin said, looking past her out the tiny porthole. "We're still the same people we were. You still want to *do,* and I guess I still just want to be."

"But what do you want to be?"

Justin was silent for a long moment. "I want to be the master of this boat," he said softly. "I want to be in charge of my own little one-man navy, and go wherever I want, whenever the wind and the tide and I agree. That's all, Kate. I want to be free. Perfectly, absolutely free."

Kate swallowed hard. It was a powerful image. She could see it in his eyes, the way they came alive when he spoke of it. And it was seductive, even to her. Maybe too seductive.

There was just one problem in Justin's vision of his future. It didn't allow room for anyone else's dream. And Kate could never be the person who would fit into his escapist fantasy. She had taken on obligations, made promises. People were counting on her to undo at least some of the damage done by a handful of small blue pills.

"I hope you get what you want," Kate said, and left him standing alone.

THIRTEEN

"Yes, Mom. Yes, I'm doing great. Really. There's nothing to worry about." Kate sat cross-legged on the floor of the upstairs hallway that evening, the phone cradled against her left ear. Her mother's voice might as well have been a million miles away. "Well, I'm sorry I didn't call when I first got here, but it was kind of crazy. Having to find a house, and all."

Here it comes, Kate thought. The question she didn't want to answer.

"Well, there's Chels, of course," Kate said slowly. "And there's a girl named Grace. She's a waitress."

Maybe that would satisfy her mother. Or not.

"No, Mom, there are three other people too." Evasion. That was the way to handle it.

"Their names?" So much for evasion. She was

only trying to protect her parents. She'd always wanted to protect them from worry, ever since Juliana. Kate had seen the unspoken fear in her parents' eyes, the unspoken question. *Might Kate also . . . ?*

"Well, there's Jus . . . Jus . . . Justine."

So much for the truth.

"And um, Alec . . . sandra. Alexandra. And of course, Connie. She's Irish."

"Anyone got some shampoo I can borrow?" Alec called from the end of the hall.

Kate clamped her hand over the phone. "Quiet! I'm on the phone!" she yelled frantically. She put the receiver back to her ear. "Who was that? That's Alexandra. She's, uh, kind of a jock, if you know what I mean. No, Mom, I don't mean she's a lesbian. She just has a low voice."

"Hi, Mrs. Quinn!" Chelsea yelled into the phone as she stepped out of her room.

"She says hi back," Kate said. "Um, I have to go, Mom. Chelsea needs me to help her move some furniture. No, Alexandra can't help, she's in the shower. Anyway, I love you and tell Daddy I love him, too."

She set down the receiver and sagged against the wall. Great. She'd lied to her mom. Massively, too, not just some little white lie. She'd invented people who didn't exist, and disinvented people who did.

"Alexandra? Justine? Connie?" Chelsea leaned against the wall, her arms folded over her chest. Her gaze was searching.

"It was the best I could do on short notice."

"I told my folks the only phone was in the hallway of our apartment building. See, that way if they call and one of the guys answers, they'll think it's one of the tenants from another apartment."

"That's good," Kate said. Chelsea could lie with the best of them. She'd been exposed, caught from time to time, but her parents never seemed to get too upset.

"Maybe it's good, maybe not," Chelsea said. "Greg's coming to see me. Tomorrow afternoon. Supposedly he'd already been planning to visit some guys he knows here, but he called right after I called my folks. I think they're sending him as a spy."

"You think he'll be upset you're living with guys?"

"I'd bet on it. But he'll get over it. You know Greg. He thinks he's God's gift to women. He's incapable of believing that any guy could be competition. What really bugs him is that I'm not back at home, where all he has to do is snap his fingers."

"Still, it'll be fun to have him around, won't it?" Kate asked as she followed Chelsea into her room.

"I don't know if it's going to be fun or not," Chelsea said. She adjusted the painting on her wall. It was one of Kate's favorite's, an oil pastel in vibrant reds and golds that Chelsea had done in art class last fall. She was glad Chelsea had thought to bring it along.

"I mean, we just got here, Kate," Chelsea went on. "It's like I've just started to live my own life for the first time, without Greg or my folks watching my every move, or B.D. bugging me about what I'm going to do with myself."

B.D. was Chelsea's brother, older by a year. He'd just completed his first year as a midshipman at Annapolis Naval Academy. B.D. was the kind of guy who'd had every detail of his life planned from the moment he popped out of the womb.

Kate stepped over Chelsea's half-unpacked suitcase. Typical Chelsea. Her walls were already covered in thumbtacked sketches of the house, the boardwalk, her housemates, even Mooch, but she still hadn't put away her clothes.

"I'll admit Greg does occasionally act like he's your father, not your boyfriend," Kate said, stepping closer to look at a rough drawing of herself.

Were her eyebrows *really* that dark? "Greg can be, sort of"—Kate paused—"overwhelming. But B.D.?"

"Oh, please, Kate. You always side with B.D." Chelsea gave her a sidelong look. "You know you've had a crush on him since you were thirteen."

"Have not," Kate said, moving on to a sketch of Justin sitting on a counter in the kitchen with Mooch at his feet. "I didn't have a crush on B.D. till I was fifteen and I saw him dressed up in a tux on his way to his junior prom."

Kate brushed aside a dirty sock and sat down on the rickety chair near the window. She propped her feet up on the windowsill and stared at the sky. Her eyes dropped to the boathouse just as Justin walked past the one small window in his loft. He was shirtless, and was carrying a book in one hand.

"Justin really ought to get some curtains," she muttered. She pulled her gaze away. "Mooch thanks you for the meatballs, by the way. Justin was there."

"I didn't want to pry." Chelsea batted her eyes. "But since you brought it up—"

"We talked. About college. About his boat. About Mooch." It was the second time she'd lied in less than five minutes.

155

"And?"

"And that was it. No big deal."

"So you don't hate him anymore?" Chelsea asked.

"I never said I hated him."

"Great, then we can stay here?"

"I didn't say *that*," Kate said quickly. "Can't you understand how I feel about this, Chels? What if you broke up with Greg? Would you want to live with him afterward?"

"Better *after* we'd broken up than before," Chelsea joked. Then she fell serious. "The thing is, I think I *do* understand," she said quietly. "And that's exactly why we should stay."

"Too bad I placed that ad in the paper today, then," Kate said.

"Ad? What ad?"

"I called the paper during my lunch break. They have a roommates-needed section."

"You could have asked me," Chelsea said resentfully. "Don't I have any say in this?"

"Of course you do. But it's not like I've made it any secret that I want to get out of this house, Chelsea."

Chelsea reached for a sketch pad and a thick, blunt-tipped pencil. "What if I *do* want to stay here?" she asked. She quickly drew a half dozen confident lines.

"You don't mean you wouldn't come with me?" Kate cried.

"I'd come," Chelsea said automatically. "You're the reason I'm here in Ocean City at all. It's just that I don't see what would be so horrible about staying here and trying to make it work."

Kate stared out the window at the boathouse. Right there. There was the answer to Chelsea's question. But for the first time, she felt a twinge of guilt. Was she being selfish, insisting that they move out?

"Look, Chelsea," she said softly. Kate wanted to explain, to set things right. "It's not just Justin. It's the fact that my parents will go nuts if they find out I'm living with three guys. You know I can't disappoint them." She sighed. "And anyway, we don't really even know any of these people."

"That's part of the fun," Chelsea said. For a moment she concentrated on her drawing. "Besides, I *like* these people."

"So do I," Kate admitted.

"Even Grace?" Chelsea asked casually.

Kate stared at the sketch of Justin. "You know what Justin said tonight? He said I shouldn't let her get to me."

Chelsea sat up straighter. She had stopped drawing. "Was that *all* he said about her?"

"He said she was complicated."

"Anything else?" Chelsea pressed.

"Why this sudden interest in Grace?"

"Just curious." Chelsea tilted her head and looked closely at Kate. Kate wasn't sure if she was just planning the next stroke of her pencil or watching Kate for a reaction.

Justin appeared in his window again. Arms braced against the sill, he stood motionless, his broad shoulders silhouetted against the soft yellow light. For all Kate knew, he was staring right at her.

"Checking out the scenery?" Chelsea asked with a grin.

Kate yanked down the window shade. "There. Satisfied?"

"That's supposed to prove to me that you're not interested in Justin?"

"You want proof? I'll give you proof. Guess who's going out to dinner with a certain older Harvard man?"

Chelsea came through with a nicely pitched scream. "That Andrew guy asked you out? You're at work one lousy day and he asks you out? This is incredible! Why didn't you tell me sooner?"

Because until a moment ago she hadn't been sure she was going to go through with it. Kate shrugged. "I don't know. I guess I've been kind of

158

preoccupied since I got home this afternoon. Besides, there's not much to tell."

"He didn't waste any time." Chelsea set aside her sketch pad. "So tell me. How cute *is* he?"

"Very."

"Kate! You're being so casual about this. A gorgeous older man who goes to Harvard asks you out after just meeting you, and this is the best you can do?"

"I hardly know the guy, Chelsea."

Chelsea made a face. "I wish I could see him for myself. Wait a minute. I've got it." She wiggled her brows suggestively. "We could double. You and Andrew and Greg and I. No. Scratch that. Andrew probably wants to have you all to himself. He'd kill you if you brought along your best friend."

"No, he wouldn't," Kate argued. "He's not like that, Chelsea. He's really very mellow. Besides, I'd like to have the moral support, to tell you the truth."

Chelsea laughed. "So would I, just in case Greg gives me a hard time about coming here for the summer."

"I'll call and ask Andrew tomorrow morning," Kate promised.

"You sound like you're going to a funeral," Chelsea teased.

Kate stood and pulled back the shade an inch. Just enough to see that the boathouse window was empty and Justin was gone.

"I'm psyched," she said quietly. "Really I am."

Chelsea held up the drawing she'd done. It showed Kate looking thoughtful, perhaps even a little wistful. "If you're psyched," Chelsea said, "I guess I'm not much of an artist."

The airport was in north Ocean City, at the very edge of development. Beyond it the dunes and sea grass took over the land, dotted here and there with a lonely fruit stand or a single roadside home.

Grace parked her Miata on the dusty little access road just outside the chain-link fence at the end of the runway. As usual, she had the top down. She snapped off the radio and listened to the sound of an airplane engine warming up. It was just a tiny two-seater prop-driven plane, and from a distance the engine sounded like an angry bee.

Grace reclined the seat so that she was looking almost straight up at the few high, thin clouds. The plane's engine revved higher, then suddenly it was airborne. It passed directly over her, blotting out the sun for a second, tossing her hair in the prop-wash.

She listened to the sound of the little plane

climbing up and away, until the droning became lost in the rustle of the wind through the sea grass. Grace closed her eyes, savoring the feel of the sun on her face.

"I figured I'd find you here."

Grace opened one eye. She'd recognized the voice instantly. "Bo, what are you doing out here?"

Bo jumped over the door and landed in the passenger seat. "I was looking for you. I went to your house, but there was no one home but some foreign guy. What's he, your new boyfriend?"

"Connor?" Grace smiled. "Hardly."

"Cool-looking house though."

Grace moved her seat back up. Bo, as usual, was dressed in oversize shorts and a black T-shirt. "What's up?" she asked. "This is a long way to come just for a chat."

"I got something to ask you. It's no big deal or anything."

"Ask away."

"I've been looking for a job."

Grace laughed out loud. "You're kidding."

"What?" Bo demanded. "Like I can't do some stupid job?"

"Of course you can, Bo. You can do anything you want to do." Grace wiped away any trace of a smile. Bo got enough criticism in his life—over his grades in school, the way he dressed, the kids he hung out with. It had made him defensive, and even more rebellious.

"Well, I can't get a job because I'm not sixteen. They all tell me I need Mom to fill out some form. Which isn't likely. She'd just tell me I had plenty of allowance."

"Then she'd tell you that working at someplace like a burger joint would bring you into contact with the wrong kind of people. Yeah, I know that lecture." *By heart,* Grace added silently. "How can I help? I can't make you sixteen."

Bo gave her his sly look. "Maybe you can. I mean, I know you can buy beer and you're not twenty-one. So obviously you have a fake ID."

Grace squirmed uncomfortably. Down toward the terminal, a passenger jet was starting its engines. "Okay. So I have a fake ID."

"How'd you get it?"

Grace sighed. "Not by very honorable means, Bo, not that there's any honorable way to get a fake ID. I swiped it out of Vicky's purse when she was here last year." Vicky was their cousin. Their twenty-two-year-old cousin who lived in California and just happened, conveniently, to look a lot like Grace.

"Cool," Bo said approvingly.

"No, Bo, it isn't cool. It's really kind of rotten,

and I'm not exactly proud of it, all right? I mean, it's no big deal for Vicky to get a new license, but that doesn't mean it was okay for me to steal."

Bo nodded, trying to pretend he was convinced. Great. She was leading her little brother onto the path of larceny. "What do you want a job so badly for, anyway?"

"Wheels, what else? When I turn sixteen, I can drive. And you know Mom will never let me drive her car."

"Dad bought me a car," Grace said. Of course, he'd done it because he'd known it would infuriate her mother.

"Dad's cool. But Mom isn't going to let him do that again. She's been freaked over this car ever since you got it."

Grace nodded. "Look, you're right. But the truth is, I don't know how to get you a fake ID. Besides, you know Mom would find out about any job you got and blow it."

Bo slumped in his seat. "I hadn't really thought about that."

"So, how's life at Mondo Condo?" Grace asked.

"She's been totally tense since you bolted, riding me all the time. Like that's news. And she and that jerk Darryl had a big fight a couple nights ago. How's life at your house?"

Grace made a back-and-forth gesture with her

hand. "Not quite as tense as home. Guess who lives down in the boathouse?"

"Who?"

"Justin."

"Justin's cool," Bo said enthusiastically. "You blew it when you guys broke up. He's the only non-jerk boyfriend you ever had." He gave her a crafty look. "And now he's right there, practically in your own house. Well, well, well."

"No, there's no *well, well, well*." She noted his look of skepticism. "At least not at the moment," she added, turning her gaze back to the plane getting ready to take off. Probably almost empty. No one *left* Ocean City on a sunny Saturday morning.

A motorcycle came bouncing and bumping along the road. The driver seemed to be going even more slowly than necessary, his eyes darting to the ground on either side of the road.

When he reached the car, he stopped, extending his blue-jeaned legs to prop up the motorcycle. He raised the opaque visor of his helmet, but left the bike's engine running. He had dark eyes and looked to be in his mid-twenties.

"Hey," he yelled. "You guys seen a purse? Kind of gold and sparkly? No strap."

Grace shook her head no. "Why? Did you lose yours?"

"Cute," the motorcyclist said. "One of my students. She claims she set her purse on the strut before we took off. I didn't see it on the runway, so I thought it might have dropped off out here."

Grace looked at him with more interest. "You a pilot?"

"Yep. I give lessons, too. David Jacob's the name. I'm in the yellow pages. Are you interested in flying?"

Grace began to answer, but the plane was warming up, its engines whining so loudly that conversation was suddenly impossible. She shrugged helplessly and he smiled back at her. David turned the bike around in a wide circle and pulled up alongside the Miata. He reached inside his leather jacket, pulled out a business card, and handed it to Grace. She nodded mutely, leaned over, and tossed it into the glove compartment. When she leaned back, he was gone, the roar of his engine lost in the shriek of the plane bearing down on them now, faster and faster, painfully loud.

"Here it comes," she yelled. She lowered the seat back again, waiting for the rush of adrenaline. The roar was deafening, shaking the very air around them, as the huge mass of polished steel lumbered overhead.

Grace felt the indefinable satisfaction she always felt at that moment, followed by the melancholy as the plane rose into the sun, carrying people off to places she had never seen, away from this town which had been their escape, and which so often felt like her prison.

FOURTEEN

Justin threaded his way through the noontime boardwalk throngs. It was busy, but what Saturday in Ocean City wasn't? Since it was a particularly beautiful day—sunny, but not too hot—the beach would be extra crowded. He was going to have his work cut out for him this afternoon.

He twisted agilely to avoid being run over by a kid racing by with a drooping cotton candy in his hand. His morning so far had been exhausting. He'd carried out one minor save, whistled hundreds of warnings and answered thousands, literally *thousands* of stupid questions. The best had been "Can't you people do anything to cool off this sand?"

"Hey, Justin! Justin!"

He cringed a little at the sound of his name. It was a girl's voice, and he knew lots of girls, none of whom he wanted to run into right at that moment.

"Justin! Here, inside the taco!"

Inside the taco?

He turned and faced what looked more or less like a big taco with large, painted-on eyes and a frilly red skirt. On closer examination, he realized that the tomato at the top of the taco was made of red-painted screen. The voice was coming from there.

"It's me, Chelsea."

"Oh, right. You mentioned you were work-ing as—"

"As Tina Taco."

"Right. Tina Taco." He peered through the screen and saw a smiling face. "That is you in there."

"Who else?"

"So what exactly do you do?" Justin asked a little awkwardly. It was tough, conversing with an oversize collection of ground beef, cheese, toma-toes, and lettuce.

"I hand out these coupons." Chelsea thrust a flyer toward him. "Buy two, get one free."

"Thanks, but I've been around long enough to know where not to eat. I was just on my way up to Floaters. It's kind of a hangout for lifeguards and locals."

"Are you implying that Tina Wina Taco tacos

are anything less than delicious?" Chelsea asked in mock anger.

"Actually, they're less than edible. I like grease as much as the next guy, but I at least like mine to be fresh."

"You think these tacos *taste* bad?" Chelsea said in a stage whisper. "I've seen how they're *made*."

"Don't tell me. I probably don't want to know." He pointed down the boardwalk. "Well, I better get going. I get only thirty minutes for lunch, and the service at Floaters is definitely laid back."

"Listen, um, do you have a minute? There's something I wanted to talk to you about. Something kind of sensitive."

Justin allowed Chelsea to pull him out of the stream of traffic, over to the boardwalk railing. "I know this is none of my business, but, well, see, yesterday, when we were all in the kitchen, I heard you call Grace *Racey*."

"Uh-huh. So?" Justin asked. "It's her nickname. She picked it up in high school. Racey Gracie."

"Well, see, when I heard you call her Racey, it kind of clicked. I mean, Kate told me everything. We are best friends and all. What I'm trying to say is, I know about the note."

"The note? What note?"

"The note on the boat."

Justin shook his head. "Not to be dense here, but what note are you talking about?"

It took Chelsea a moment to answer. "The one that said"—she lowered her voice to a whisper—"'You're an amazing lover, signed Racey.'"

Justin's mind flew into overdrive. Then in a flash it all fell into place. "She saw *that* note? Kate saw that note from Grace to me?"

"On your boat."

Justin covered his face with his hand. Kate had seen the note. No wonder she'd been so enraged that last time.

He let out a long sigh.

He leaned closer to Chelsea's tomato screen. "You're telling me that Kate knows about me and Grace?"

"She knows about you and someone named Racey," Chelsea corrected. "Kate was already gone yesterday when you called Grace by her nickname."

"And you haven't told her?"

"No, I haven't told her. Listen, I think you and Kate have some unfinished business between you. But if Kate finds out Grace was the one you were, uh, involved with, she'll bolt. And I'll probably have to bolt with her."

Justin gazed off toward the water. Somewhere his mind registered the fact that his lunch half-hour was ticking away. But he'd lost his appetite anyway.

"Look, Grace and I were close, all right," he said. "But it was over before I even met Kate."

Chelsea put her hands on her hips—which was more or less the spot where her taco met her skirt. "Then why did you sleep with Grace," she demanded, "*while* you were seeing Kate?"

Justin sighed. "It was one of those things, you know? Kate and I had been fighting. It was clear to me she was blowing me off, and I just happened to run into Grace, and I was depressed and had a bottle of wine in my boat, and—" He shrugged again. Right, Justin. Try explaining that to Kate—*I slept with Grace to take my mind off you.*

"Listen," Chelsea said, "this isn't my business, so I'm not going to say anything to Kate. But she remembers that note, believe me, and if she hears you call Grace Racey, she'll put it all together. A word to the wise."

"Thanks," Justin said quietly.

He gave Chelsea a wave and started off toward Floaters, but a check of his watch told him there was no way he could make it there and back in time. Reluctantly he turned back toward his chair. Maybe he could get Alec to sneak him out a sandwich later.

So, Kate had seen that note. Not that it changed anything, really. Still, he would have to resolve all this sooner or later and tell her the truth. Even though they were through, he didn't want Kate thinking he was a liar.

Suddenly he stopped and groaned out loud as the realization hit him. It wasn't just that Kate didn't know about Grace. Grace didn't know about Kate, either.

Too bad the boat wasn't ready. Now would be a great time to head to the Bahamas.

"Hold the applause, folks," Alec called as he and Justin entered the living room. Justin laughed as Alec, hands clasped over his head and humming the theme from *Rocky,* trotted into the dining room.

Grace, dressed in a man's blue oxford shirt and nothing else, was ironing her waiter uniform on the dining-room table. "Alec playing with his invisible friends again?" she asked.

Justin leaned against the door and smiled. "We had a couple of rescues today and he thinks he's some kind of conquering hero."

Chelsea came in from the kitchen, wiping her hands on a dish towel. There was a tall black guy with her. "Who got rescued?" Chelsea asked.

"Justin pulled in a couple kids who got

172

caught in the undertow. We had a serious rip today," Alec said, hopping onto the edge of the table. "And I"—he paused long enough to rub his knuckles on his chest—"saved the life of one Mrs. Lucille Zweigart of Ontario, Canada."

Connor looked up from the book he was reading. "Do you get extra points for saving a foreigner?"

"She was blue," Alec said, shaking his head. "Took five minutes of mouth-to-mouth to get her going."

It was more like thirty seconds, actually, but who was Justin to argue? He knew how it was. When you were trying to blow life back into somebody, every minute was a century. "Rookie did all right for himself," he said.

"Yes, nothing like a bit of the ol' mouth-to-mouth," Connor added.

"Mrs. Zweigart is sixty-four, Riordan," Alec shot back.

Connor shrugged. "Myself, I'm partial to older women."

"Shut up, Connor, you sleaze." Chelsea tossed the dish towel and landed a direct hit on his face. "Well, congratulations, guys. This is really cool. I'll bet we're the only house in O.C. with two actual heroes in it. Oh, I nearly forgot. You guys haven't met Greg yet. This is Greg, my boyfriend from back home. Greg, meet Alec and Justin."

Greg shook their hands, gave them both a quick up-and-down. "Congrats," he said in a not particularly impressed voice. "I gather you're both lifeguards. Well, if you gotta work, I guess there are worse gigs than staring at miles of flesh all summer." If the gold Rolex on Greg's wrist and the BMW parked out front were any indication, Justin thought, Greg didn't know a whole lot about work. He certainly hadn't paid for that car by flipping burgers at McDonald's.

"Guarding's a great job," Alec said with feeling, meeting Justin's eyes. Justin nodded. It *was* a great job, despite all the grunt work and regulations and paperwork. He knew why Alec was so psyched. After his first rescue, he'd been high for a week.

Greg nudged Chelsea. "Beats dressing up like a burrito, at least."

"Taco," Chelsea corrected through clenched teeth.

"Hi, everyone, what's going on?"

Justin turned to see Kate coming down the stairs. She was wearing a dress, short and black and clingy, the kind that left just enough to the imagination.

Kate sat down on one of the dining-room chairs. As she passed, she left a subtle trail of perfume in her wake, a spicy-sweet scent that made Justin remember things about last summer that he'd been trying hard to forget. And things about that kiss in the boathouse that he hadn't even begun to forget.

"Justin and Alec are heroes, Kate," Chelsea said. "They each rescued people today."

"That's great," Kate said. "Congratulations."

"All in the line of duty," Alec said, but he was grinning like a kid. "Justin's one up, though. He had two."

"He's quite the man of action," Kate said.

Grace unplugged the iron. "Big date?" she asked as she passed Kate.

"She's going out with this guy from Safe Seas," Chelsea volunteered quickly. "Greg and I are doubling with them."

Justin rolled his eyes. "So, what's on the agenda? A dinner of granola and sprouts while you discuss recycling?" Justin knew he should keep his mouth shut, but the words had come out before he could stop them.

"You'd better get dressed, Chels," Kate said coolly. "Andrew will be here soon."

"Well, wherever you go, just remember one thing," Grace said as she pulled her black bow tie out of her shirt pocket. "Tip twenty percent or die."

"I'm not sure where we're going," Kate said. "Andrew just said to dress up and plan on a great view."

Justin suppressed the growing tide of irrational anger. *Cut it out, Garrett,* he told himself. He was being a jerk. Kate's love life was her own business.

"Don't forget curfew," Grace warned Kate sweetly. She paused as she passed Alec and gave him a kiss on the cheek. "You could save me anytime, Alec," she said.

When she got to Justin, she eased close, her shirt soft against his bare chest. "My hero," she said, and brushed her lips against his.

Justin glanced over at Chelsea, who was sending him warning looks like daggers.

"My turn," Connor called. "Over here, Grace, darling."

"What exactly was your act of heroism?" Grace demanded.

Connor sighed heavily. "I ran out of tea bags this morning and was forced to drink half a cup of Chelsea's coffee."

"No dice, Connor. I drank two cups myself."

"Hey," Justin called as Grace headed back toward her room, "haven't I seen that shirt somewhere before?"

"I found it in the dryer," Grace said. "Yours?"

Justin nodded.

"So much the better," Grace said with a sly smile before disappearing.

"While we're on the subject of borrowing," Alec said, "did one of you women swipe my razor this morning?"

"Oops." Chelsea winced. "Sorry. Mine was shot, and I couldn't find Kate's."

Alec pointed to the Band-Aid on his neck. "I nearly sliced open my jugular, Chelsea."

"What are you whining about?" Chelsea demanded. "I found my ten-dollar-a-bottle shampoo in the upstairs guy bathroom."

"Don't look at *me*," Alec protested.

"Why is it, do you suppose," Connor asked from the couch, "they felt compelled to put sheep placenta in that concoction?"

Justin glanced over at Kate. She gave him a look he didn't understand. Annoyance? Jealousy?

"Have a good time tonight," he told her as he started to leave. He'd meant it to sound sincere. Even to his ears it didn't.

"Hey, Justin," Alec called. "I thought we were going to do a little celebrating around town—"

"Later," Justin said. Much later. Crowds or not, O.C. was the kind of town where you eventually ran into everyone you knew. And he was in no mood to run into Kate on her date.

Not tonight, not when she was wearing that dress and that perfume and looking so damn good.

FIFTEEN

No doubt about it, this was turning into the date from hell. Not that Andrew wasn't a great guy. He was. And he looked fantastic. The suit-and-tie thing really worked on him.

He'd been a real sweetheart when Kate had asked if Chelsea and Greg could come along too. Unfortunately, Kate had violated one of the Ten Dating Commandments: Thou shalt never double with a couple on the verge of splitting up.

Chelsea and Greg had been bickering all evening. Just little things, but it really made it hard for Kate and Andrew to carry on an intelligent conversation.

Of course, intelligent conversation was a lot easier when you could at least remember the name of your date. When your date's name was Andrew, and you said something along the lines of *Isn't this a great view, Justin*, it could really put a damper on things—especially when your housemate chose to react to your little slip of the tongue by knocking her water glass into your date's lap.

But Andrew was a trouper. He'd laughed it off, made some joke about how was it going to look when he left the restaurant with a big wet spot in his lap. He even pretended he hadn't heard the Justin thing.

Kate was acting like a real idiot. It wasn't as if this was her first date in history. It wasn't as if she'd never eaten in a nice restaurant before. But this particular nice restaurant was The Claw. Why couldn't Andrew have made reservations at one of the other dozen or so nice restaurants in Ocean City?

At least Grace wasn't their waitress. They'd been spared that awkward scene. But she had to pass their table often to pick up drinks at the bar. And every time she passed, Kate flashed back to that afternoon, when Grace had kissed Justin.

An innocent, friendly kiss, that was all. Kate kept telling herself that. Grace had kissed Alec, too. But there'd been something about the way she'd lingered just a millisecond or two past a just-friendly peck with Justin that made Kate wonder if there was something more there. And *that* made her wonder why she was wondering. What did she care if Grace was interested in Justin—

"Four virgins."

Kate looked up with a start. It was Grace, holding a tray of pink drinks. How long had she been standing there?

"Our sex life is really none of your business, Grace," Kate began.

"The drinks, Kate," Chelsea interrupted. "She's talking about the drinks. Virgin means they don't have any alcohol in them."

"Four virgin strawberry margaritas," Grace said, dropping a glass in front of each of them with practiced ease. "On me."

"Thanks, Grace," Chelsea said, taking a sip from her straw. "Are you sure there isn't a little tequila in these? They taste great."

"No, I made sure they were virgins." Grace batted her eyes. "After all, I didn't want to have to schedule a vote."

That summed up Grace, Kate reflected as she watched her walk away. She'd done something nice, bringing them the drinks, then delivered them with a barb.

"What was that all about?" Andrew asked.

"She's one of our new housemates," Kate said with a shrug. "We had a little run-in about house rules."

"Uh-oh," Greg said, leaning back in his chair and shaking his head. "Watch out. When Kate has a run-in with someone, it's more like a head-on collision." He nudged Chelsea. "Remember that time she staged a sit-in in the cafeteria because they were using Styrofoam plates? I was so P.O.ed at her. I thought I was going to starve."

"Well, I was proud of her," Chelsea countered. "She got the school board to switch."

"I'm impressed," Andrew said, and Kate had the feeling he meant it.

"So what was the problem with this Grace?" Greg asked.

"She wanted to bring beer into the house, and when Chelsea and I and another one of our roommates wanted to discuss it, Grace seemed to take it personally. No biggie."

"Are you still trying to move out?" Andrew asked.

"Yep," Kate said. "But we haven't found anything yet. I put an ad in the paper, but so far, no takers."

"I say they should move back home tomorrow," Greg volunteered. "Take it easy this summer, instead of sweating it out at some taco joint."

"Greg, can we please drop the subject?" Chelsea complained. "I can't come home. All my stuff is here, and Kate is here. . . ."

"I just don't see why you're bothering, baby. You're making minimum wage. You'll be lucky if you can cover your expenses." Greg put on a pouty expression. "At least if you want to work, work at home, where you can be with me."

Chelsea reached for her margarita and stared straight ahead, her eyes molten. Kate fumed with her in sisterly solidarity. This pushy, possessive side of Greg always got on Kate's nerves. But what bugged her more was the way Chelsea tolerated it. Chelsea had never been big on confrontation. Deciding to come with Kate to Ocean City against the wishes of her parents—and very much against Greg's wishes—had been about the most confrontational thing she'd ever done.

It wasn't that Chelsea didn't get her way when she wanted to. It was just that she favored more subtle methods, and that sometimes frustrated Kate. Kate badly wanted to tell Greg where to get off, but it was Chelsea's relationship, not hers.

Not that she was exactly an expert at handling relationships.

"I meant to tell you, I heard about a two-bedroom bayside condo for rent," Andrew said, changing the subject. "A friend of mine knows the owner. Want me to check it out for you?"

"Absolutely," Kate said, watching as Grace

moved past, a tray loaded with dishes held high on one hand over her head.

"You won't need a two bedroom, Kate," Greg said firmly. He reached for Chelsea's hand and gave it a kiss. Chelsea made a face. "Not after I've talked Teensy Taco here into coming home."

"Maybe you should try letting her live her own life, Greg," Kate suggested.

"It's so flattering having you two fighting over me," Chelsea said, sending Kate an I'll-take-care of-it-myself look.

Andrew cleared his throat. "It'll probably be a while till our order comes," he said to Kate. "Why don't you and I head downstairs? They have a great dance floor."

"It's way too early for anybody to be dancing, isn't it?" Kate asked. The truth was, she was a lousy dancer.

"There's a deejay on until ten. Then the band starts." Andrew pushed back his chair. "Come on," he urged.

"Let's hit the floor too," Greg suggested.

"Greg, I kind of think they want to be alone," Chelsea replied.

"Come on," Andrew said, reaching for Kate's arm.

Reluctantly she stood. Chelsea and Greg would just have to duke it out without a referee.

"Sorry," Andrew said as he led her down the winding staircase to the lower level of the restaurant. "I needed a break from the Simpsons."

Kate laughed. "You're really being cool about it," she said as they stepped into the dark bar. The deejay was keeping the early music mellow. A few couples sat near the wide windows, watching the first stars materialize over the ocean. The dance floor was empty.

"May I have this dance?" Andrew asked as a lazy, familiar tune came over the sound system.

"Maybe we should just sit," Kate said, taking a step backward. "No one's dancing."

But Andrew had already slipped his arm around her back and eased her onto the sleek wooden floor. "I'm a lousy dancer," Kate whispered.

"That's okay," Andrew said, pulling her a little closer. "I'm not."

They began to sway, a gentle slow dance that even Kate could manage. Andrew moved with such certainty that she began to relax, and after a while she even forgot that they were all alone on the dance floor. She leaned her head onto the scratchy fabric of his jacket. This was nice. In Andrew's arms, it was easy to stop thinking about Grace and Justin and Chelsea and Greg and the whole rest of the planet.

"When I asked you out, I had no idea what a campus radical I was getting involved with," Andrew said.

Kate looked up and smiled. "Scared?" she teased.

"Quite the contrary. I'm looking forward to voting for you for president someday."

"Good." Kate rested her head on his jacket again. "Because I'm planning to run."

"Thought so."

She could feel Andrew's hand hard on her back, feel his lips just brushing her hair as he spoke. Nice. This was getting even nicer.

"Here's the plan," Kate murmured. "I go to Columbia, get a B.A. in political science with a minor in ecology, follow it up with law school, intern summers with Congress, practice environmental law, do a couple terms in the Senate, then become the first woman president." She couldn't help laughing at herself. "What do you think?"

"I think you're incredible."

"Not crazy?"

"Not at all," Andrew said.

"Not . . . too ambitious?"

"I like that about you, Kate." Andrew stroked her hair. "You've got brains, and ideals, and you want to do something with them. Nothing wrong with that." He looked down at her, smiling gently.

"There's this person," she said, "this guy, actually. He says I'm too caught up in doing, and not enough in being."

"Well, this person—this guy—has a point, I suppose," Andrew said, pulling her just a little closer. "But I'd rather try to change the world than just stand on the sidelines and throw up my hands."

Kate closed her eyes. She felt calm and safe in Andrew's arms. He was gorgeous and brilliant and older, and unlike Justin, he liked her just the way she was.

"Hey," he whispered. "I forgot something. Remember when I said that about being brainy and idealistic?"

"Change your mind?"

"Nope. I forgot to mention that you just happen to be beautiful." He let his lips brush her forehead in a whisper of a kiss. "Very beautiful."

"Really?"

"Let's just put it this way. You made work very difficult yesterday. As a matter of fact, you made sleep very difficult."

The first tune segued seamlessly into another. Kate kept her eyes closed. She stopped caring about whether she could dance or not, or whether people were staring at them. She didn't even care if Greg and Chelsea had killed each other by now. And when the song ended and Andrew leaned down and kissed her lightly on the lips, she stopped caring about much of anything at all.

"Thanks," Andrew whispered as he slowly pulled away.

"Thank you," Kate whispered back.

He kissed her again more deeply, and Kate felt a little jolt of electricity skate down her spine. Suddenly she realized they were standing all alone on the dance floor. Gently she pulled away, but Andrew kept his arms circled tightly around her waist.

"We should probably get going," Kate said. "It should be safe up there by now. I imagine Chelsea's worn Greg down."

When they reached the top of the stairs, Kate wasn't surprised to see that Greg was sitting back, looking confused and defeated, while Chelsea was expounding at length on some topic, waving her arms for emphasis.

Grace was at the bar, placing a round of drinks on a small tray. Suddenly a pretty, middle-aged woman brushed past Kate, making a bee-line for Grace.

"Where is he, Grace?" she hissed, just loudly enough for Kate and one or two other bystanders to hear. Kate couldn't help staring.

The woman grabbed Grace's arm. "Tell me!" she snapped.

Was it Grace's mother? They did look a lot alike—same almond eyes, same high cheekbones. But where Grace's eyes were set in steely determination, the older woman's were both angry and strangely unfocused.

"What are you talking about, Mother?" Grace demanded, shaking off the woman's arm.

"Bo. Where's Bo? He's gone, disappeared."

Grace went pale. "Bo? What do you mean, gone? For how long?"

Her mother seemed taken aback by the question. "I'm not sure. Since last night, or maybe this morning."

"You don't *know*?" Grace cried. She rolled her eyes, glanced around the bar, then pulled her mother toward her and began to whisper.

"We should go," Kate said to Andrew, but she couldn't seem to take her eyes off Grace. The cool sophistication had evaporated the instant her mother had said the name Bo. Suddenly, inexplicably, Grace had looked vulnerable.

"There's our food now," Andrew said, nodding toward their table.

"You go ahead," Kate said. "I'll be right there."

Hesitantly she crossed the bar. Grace and her mother were still huddled together, talking in low, heated voices. Suddenly her mother turned and bolted from the room. Grace sagged, then reached over and lifted one of the drinks from her tray. In one swift move, she tossed it back and swallowed it. Then she set the empty glass in a bus tray.

"Anton," she called. "I still need that bourbon rocks."

The bartender looked at her in confusion. "I could have sworn I poured that drink already." With a shrug, he poured another and placed it on Grace's tray.

Grace turned and noticed Kate for the first time. For a split second, Grace looked guilty, even fearful. Then the mask came down again. She picked up her tray and walked away without a word.

SIXTEEN

She was going to kill him. That was, if she ever found him, she was going to kill him. No, first she'd kill her mother. Her mother, who was too full of self-pity and self-loathing and eighty-proof scotch to even know if her son had come home last night.

Grace screeched to a halt in front of the house. She checked her watch. It was nearly eleven thirty. She'd tried like crazy to get someone to cover her station so she could get out early and go looking for Bo, but her manager had vetoed the idea. As it was, she'd blown off cleaning up and rushed out the door as soon as her last table had taken the hint.

Her mother had already called the police, of course, but in O.C., runaways were a dime a dozen, and Bo wouldn't even officially *be* a run-

190

away until he'd been gone twenty-four hours. Grace knew she had to start looking on her own. But for some reason, her first thought had been to head home and find Justin. She wasn't sure why. He was calm, good in a crisis, he knew the town backward and forward, he knew Bo. Those were the things she told herself. But mostly, she knew, she just wanted someone to tell her Bo would be okay. That it wasn't her fault he'd run away. That this hard, icy spot in her stomach would go away, and that Bo would be found, safe and sound and his usual cocky self.

She dashed up the front steps and tossed her purse on the porch swing, along with her apron full of uncounted tips. The living room was empty, but she thought she heard voices coming from the kitchen.

Someone stepped into the dark dining room. Justin. Before he could even say anything, she ran to him and buried her head on his chest. "Justin," she sobbed, "Bo's gone and it's all my fault—"

"Shh, Racey." He kissed her forehead, cupped her head in his hands and made her look at him. "It's okay. He's here."

"Here?" She didn't understand.

"In the kitchen. He showed up about ten minutes ago. I called you at work, but you'd already left."

"He's all right?"

"He's fine. Just a little shook up."

"Shook up? How the hell does he think I feel?"

She started toward the kitchen, but Justin grabbed her. "He needs a friend right now, Grace."

"Yeah, don't we all."

The moment of relief was gone, and in the hole left behind there was rage. She ran into the kitchen. Bo was by the refrigerator. "Hey," he said. "Meet your new roommate."

She stalked over to him, pulled back her hand. "Grace," Justin warned, but it was too late. She let it fly and hit Bo on the side of his face, hard.

The red handprint formed slowly on his cheek. Bo stared at her, confused. "That's a mean right hook you got, Gracie," he said at last. "Learn that from Mom?"

That was all it took. Instantly the tears came. "Bo, I'm sorry," she sobbed. "I was just so scared when she told me you'd disappeared. I thought—" She pulled him to her and gave him a hard hug.

"Hey," Bo said, breaking free. "Take it easy."

"I'm sorry. It's just that I felt so responsible."

"You?" Bo gave a short laugh.

"For leaving you alone with her."

Bo opened the fridge and pulled out a root

beer. "Okay if I snag one of these?" he asked.

"Sure." Grace sat down at the table next to Justin. He gave her a reassuring wink. But when she looked back at Bo's face, she felt horrified all over again. "I can't believe I hit you like that," she moaned. "It was just like her."

"You'll never be like her," Bo said matter-of-factly. He sat down with them, gulped down the root beer, and let out an ear-splitting belch.

"Told you he was okay," Justin said.

"Where have you been all this time?" Grace asked. She was starting to calm down now, to feel back in control.

"I stayed with Billy Chapman last night. I'm still trying to get a job so I can make it on my own. You know—like you and Justin."

"I was a lot older than you when I moved into my own place," Justin pointed out. "And my mom had moved to Vermont and gotten remarried. I had a good reason."

"Yeah, well, my mom's a drunk," Bo said dryly. "That a good enough reason for you?"

"Bo," Grace said gently, reaching for his hand. "Did something happen?"

Bo shrugged. "She's just turned into a major fascist. It was bad enough before, but now that you're out of the picture . . . I just can't hack it anymore."

"So she hasn't hurt you, nothing like that?"

Bo shrugged. "Just the usual. She tried to take my skateboard away. She locked it in her closet, so I busted it open and split."

Grace sighed. This was all so complicated. She wasn't a mother. Maybe Bo had done something to deserve the punishment. Maybe their mother had been in the right, for once. That was one of the terrible things about having a parent with a drinking problem—you began to assume they were never in the right.

And Bo could be a little wild at times. Nothing serious, it seemed to her, but what did she know about disciplining a fifteen-year-old? She'd never exactly followed the rules herself. Had she ever made curfew, even once? Still, did she want to encourage her brother to repeat her own mistakes?

"So," she paused, tracing circles on the kitchen table, "what are your plans now?"

Bo looked up hopefully, not at her, but at Justin. "Grace," Justin said softly, "how about you and I go have a chat on the porch?"

She cast Bo a doubtful look. "So you got to Justin first, huh? Figure he'll butter me up for whatever it is you want?"

Bo grinned his lopsided smile. It was way too endearing for his own good. "He's a guy, Grace. We guys understand things."

"Things," she repeated. "Uh-huh." She shook her head and stood. "Oh, all right," she said. "Come on, Justin. Let's go sit on the porch while you manipulate me."

Bo grinned. "Sounds like fun. Can I watch?"

She followed Justin onto the porch. They sat on the swing. The night was warm, soft on her skin. The darkness soothed her, or maybe it was the feel of Justin's arm around her shoulders. He felt so solid, so centered, and he made her feel that way too.

"Thanks," she whispered.

"For what?"

She shrugged. It was hard to explain. "For being there. And for knowing me. Hardly anyone does, I guess."

"I like a challenge."

She eased the swing back and forth with her foot. A weather front stretched a line of clouds arrow-straight across the sky. Moonlight turned the edges silver. "He wants to stay here for a while, doesn't he?"

Justin nodded.

"What did you tell him?"

"I told him I ran away twice when I was fifteen."

"Great. As a role model, you basically suck. Unfortunately, so do I." She laid her hand on his thigh. His jeans were soft as flannel with wear, the muscles beneath surprisingly hard. "I didn't mean that. You're a great role model for Bo. He adores you. And it means a lot to him, since Dad isn't around much anymore—" Suddenly she stopped. As if Justin didn't know what it was like not to have a dad around.

Justin smiled. "The kid even offered to pay rent. He doesn't want to take advantage of you, and he's afraid that part of the reason you moved out was to get away from your annoying brother."

"But I told him—"

"Oh, I think he knows the real reason, deep down. He just wants a little more freedom." Justin leaned back, shook his head. "I told him it's not all it's cracked up to be, being on your own. He wasn't buying it."

"So what do I do?"

"Let him stay a few days till things cool off. Call Ellen so she can relax. My guess is he'll go back eventually." He laughed softly. "I always did."

"But what about the others?"

"I wouldn't worry too much. Nobody's going to mind having Bo around for a few days. He's a good kid."

Grace hesitated. "I don't know. It's kind of like I'm springing something new on everyone, without really asking. And after the beer flap . . . I'd rather not provoke another hassle, especially with Kate."

"So, ask everyone what they think. And don't assume Kate will object. She'll be cool about it, if you explain the circumstances."

Grace noticed a strangely proprietary tone in Justin's voice. Was he starting to become interested in Kate? So far he'd seemed indifferent, maybe even a little unfriendly toward her. "How do you know she'll be cool?"

Justin shrugged. "I just do."

She slipped her hand in his. The warm strength was reassuring. "What about my mom?" she asked. "What if she freaks?"

"You can handle her."

"I'm glad you're so confident. I wish I were." She paused. There were footsteps on the sidewalk, a high-heeled *click-click.*

Grace stood up, sending the swing into a gentle back-and-forth motion. "Okay, I'm just going to explain it to everyone. Promise you'll give me backup if I need it?"

"Always have."

It was true. Grace leaned down and gave Justin a quick kiss. He didn't return it, but he didn't turn away, either. "I think you're pretty great, you know that?" she whispered.

"Same here, Racey."

Grace walked across the porch to see who was coming. It was Kate, but she had stopped. She was standing on the sidewalk under a streetlamp, staring at Grace. After a moment she turned away and headed down toward the water, disappearing quickly in the shadows.

"What are you looking at?" Justin asked.

"Kate," Grace said. "She just gave me this death look and took off."

"Took off? Why would she do that?"

"Who knows?"

Justin sat up straight, his eyes narrowed, but he didn't say anything. He seemed to be peering intently into the darkness at the water's edge.

"Oh well," Grace said with a sigh. "I don't see how her night could have been any worse than mine."

SEVENTEEN

Kate stopped at the top of the stairs, her breath coming in sharp gasps. She willed them to stop, but the sobs kept coming. She'd been down by the water, crying, when she'd seen Justin heading down from the porch. Justin. The last person on earth she wanted to see right then, with the possible exception of Grace.

She'd run around to the side entrance of the house, nearly slipping on the wet grass, and dashed inside and up the stairs, praying she didn't run into Grace on the way. Praying she didn't run into *anyone* on the way.

To her relief, Chelsea's door was closed. That meant she was already home.

Kate placed a trembling hand on the doorknob. Thank God Chelsea had come with Kate to Ocean City. She couldn't remember when she'd needed her best friend more. Chelsea would be there for her, as she always was. She'd tell her they could pack up and move tomorrow, that Justin was a jerk and that Grace was a bitch and that Andrew showed a lot of potential. She'd make all this hurt and anger go away.

Or, at very least, she'd get angry too. That was almost as good.

"Chelsea?" Kate called.

"Come on in. My lord and master's gone to his friends' house."

Kate stepped into Chelsea's bedroom and closed the door behind her. There was no easy way to say it.

"It's Grace," she whispered.

Chelsea was standing by her mirror, unzipping her dress. "Can you believe the gall of that man? I told Greg—" Suddenly she stopped cold, slowly cocking her head to one side. "What did you say?"

Kate sat on the edge of Chelsea's bed. "I said that Grace is the one."

Chelsea frowned. "The one?"

"Grace slept with Justin," Kate blurted, her voice raw from crying. "She's Racey. She's the one who was with him on his boat. The one who—"

"I'm sorry, Kate." Chelsea settled onto the bed beside Kate and put her arm around her shoulder.

"I can't believe it. I can't believe it's her." Kate wiped her nose with a mangled Kleenex.

"Well, I guess O.C. is a pretty cozy place in the off-season," Chelsea offered. "And there's only the one high school and all. It's not really that big a coincidence, their having been . . . together."

Kate pulled back to stare at her friend. Chelsea was supposed to be shocked. Indignant. Morally outraged. "You don't seem all that surprised," Kate said suspiciously.

Chelsea stood abruptly. She walked over to her dresser and tossed one of her gold hoop earrings into her jewelry box. "I sort of knew already."

Her words hung in the air. Kate waited for them to register, but she seemed to be going numb.

"You sort of knew?" she said at last. "That Grace was Racey? You *sort of* knew that?"

"I overheard Justin call her that once."

Kate shook her head uncomprehendingly. "You knew, and you didn't tell me?"

"Look, I knew you'd overreact," Chelsea said. Her voice was tinged with guilt. "Besides, supposedly it's all over between you and Justin. So this is really no big deal, right?"

"Chelsea," Kate said plaintively, "you're supposed to be my best friend. If you really thought it was no big deal, you would have told me. Why didn't you? Why would you let me go on walking around like nothing was happening while the girl who seduced my boyfriend was laughing behind my back?"

"I don't think she is," Chelsea said. "I've been watching Grace, and I don't think she knows about you any more than you knew about her. Besides, Justin said it was over a long time ago between them."

"He said . . . you talked this over with him?" Kate cried. She jumped to her feet. "You *discussed* this with Justin? What did you do, warn him to be careful what he said around me?"

Chelsea winced, confirming the truth.

"*Why*, Chelsea? You're my best friend in the world. Why wouldn't you tell me—" Suddenly it hit her. "It's the house," she whispered. "You were afraid if I found out the truth, I'd be even more determined to move out right away."

"Look, I'm sorry, Kate." Chelsea stared at her reflection in the dresser mirror. "I apologize. I didn't realize you'd get so mad."

"And now you think you can just apologize and that's it?" Kate threw up her hands. "How am I supposed to trust you, Chelsea? You've been manipulating me for your own selfish reasons, instead of—"

"*My* own selfish reasons?" Chelsea spun around, eyes blazing. "How about your selfish reasons? Why should I have to give up my first house just because you have a little problem with Justin? *I'm* selfish? What about you?"

Chelsea reached down, yanked off one of her new leather sandals, and flung it across the room in a burst of fury. It whizzed past Kate's head, landing in the wastebasket with a thud.

Kate stared from the wastebasket, to Chelsea's bare foot, to Chelsea's face, set in grim determination. This wasn't Chelsea. This was Chelsea on steroids. "Did something happen with Greg?" Kate asked. "Are you sure this is just about the house?"

"This is about everything." Chelsea yanked off her other shoe. Kate flinched, but this time Chelsea just tossed it into her closet. "I don't want to move out," she said more quietly. "I like this house. I get great light in this room. I look out my window and see things I want to draw and paint. It feels . . . right to me."

"You wouldn't even be here if it weren't for me," Kate whispered. Suddenly, instead of anger, she felt horribly, intensely alone. "This was supposed to be our summer together, Chelsea. Yours and mine."

"I know you're right. But you and I aren't

Siamese twins. We're not joined at the hip. I can make my own decisions."

"You should have told me. You should have told me straight out."

"I don't do very well when I tell people things straight out," Chelsea admitted quietly.

Kate felt her anger ebb away. It was slippery and tough to hang on to, hard as she tried. She understood Chelsea too well. She *did* manipulate people, but maybe it really was because she didn't think she had a choice. Now, watching her friend try to change herself, a tiny part of Kate was rooting for Chelsea, despite her anger.

They fell into silence. Kate sat on the bed, staring out the window. Chelsea changed into a pair of gym shorts and a tank top. Then she began to purposefully unpack the odds and ends still in her suitcase.

Finally Kate said it. "I'm still moving out," she whispered. "Won't you please come with me?"

Chelsea paused. She bit her lip, clearly wavering. Then she swallowed hard. "You want me to answer straight out?" she asked. "No, Kate. I'm staying."

Kate got up slowly and walked back to her room. She closed the door, lay down on her bed, and buried her head in her pillow. Only then, when she was sure no one else could hear her, did she let the tears flow freely again.

Grace opened one eye and stared at the clock. Why would she have set it for such an early hour? She wasn't due at The Claw for eight hours.

Oh yeah. Suddenly it hit her. Bo.

Breakfast was the one time when most of the housemates seemed to be around. And Bo's presence out on the living-room couch would probably require some explanation.

She found the bathroom unoccupied and quickly brushed her teeth, washed her face, and tried to fully regain consciousness.

Alec and Chelsea were the only ones in the kitchen when Grace arrived. Alec was making oatmeal, something he'd obviously never done before, judging from the number of times he went back to check the directions. Chelsea, who was wearing a pretty, conservative-looking blue dress and leather pumps, seemed unusually sullen as she carefully buttered an English muffin.

"Hi, kids," Grace said, heading directly for the coffee machine and loading the basket. "Going to a funeral, Chelsea?"

"No, Mass. It's Sunday."

"So it is," Grace acknowledged.

"You know anything about cooking?" Alec

asked plaintively. "I don't think this stuff is supposed to be so runny."

"Sorry. I'm not much good in the kitchen."

Connor came in next, wearing a plaid bathrobe over boxer shorts and unlaced boots. He spotted Alec struggling with the oatmeal. "Sick of my doughnuts already, eh? Good. That shows you have some taste." He peered over Alec's shoulder. "Good lord, what is that mess?"

"Oatmeal?" Alec answered tentatively.

"Did you measure at all?"

"I couldn't find a measuring cup," Alec admitted. Connor stepped in to help, muttering something about Yanks who couldn't figure out how to boil water.

Kate appeared in the doorway. When she caught sight of Grace, she seemed to freeze, her cheeks pale, her lips set in a grim line.

Just then Justin pushed open the screen door to the kitchen. As he stepped inside, his gaze flickered from Kate to Grace, then seemed to shift longingly back toward the door.

Kate stalked toward the refrigerator. "I didn't expect to see you up this early, Grace," she said icily. "But then, you're full of surprises."

What is bugging her? Grace wondered. For that matter, why did Justin look like he was ready to bolt for cover? And why did Chelsea look so down? The one person in this house you could count on to be cheerful was Chelsea, and she looked as if she'd just lost her best friend.

"I had something I wanted to mention to everyone," Grace began tentatively, "and it's easiest to catch everyone in the morning. Much as I personally disapprove of morning."

The joke went nowhere.

"I hope you're going to explain why there's a person snoring in our living room," Kate said, carefully keeping her attention focused on the melon she was slicing open.

Stay cool, Grace told herself.

"That's my little brother, Bo," Grace answered evenly. "He's going to be staying with me for a while."

"A while?" Kate asked. "As in hours? Days? Months?"

"I don't know, exactly," Grace said.

"How old is he?" Chelsea asked, speaking up for the first time.

"Fifteen."

"Why isn't he at home?" Kate asked pointedly.

Grace hesitated. It was a fair question, an inevitable question. "He's having some problems at home."

"He's fifteen," Kate said, chopping the melon into little cubes. "Fifteen-year-old guys always have problems at home. It's part of growing up."

"I didn't," Alec said.

"You wouldn't," Connor muttered.

"Look, these are not normal, everyday problems—" Grace began.

"Kate, the kid just needs a little time to decompress, that's all," Justin said, but his words had no effect on her. On the contrary, Kate seemed to be chopping the melon with a certain ferocity. It was bizarre. Whatever her faults, Kate had struck Grace as the soul of reason and fairmindedness. Now she looked as if she was ready to grab a gun and go on a shooting spree.

"Listen, Chelsea signed a lease. People can't just bring in extra roommates whenever they want," Kate continued in an agitated voice.

Justin sighed loudly. "Look, Kate, he's just a kid who's having a tough time. In a couple of days, he'll be ready to go back home."

"This is a matter for people living in this house. You live in the boathouse, Justin," Kate snapped, hacking away at her melon cubes. "As you've made abundantly clear, what you do there is your own business. In your boathouse"— she shot him a laser-hot glare—"*or* in your boat." Suddenly the knife slipped and Kate nicked her finger. A tiny line of blood appeared and she stuck the finger in her mouth.

"Why do you care about this so much?" Chelsea asked sarcastically. "You're moving out."

Grace frowned. Chelsea sniping at Kate? Kate sniping at Justin? Something was definitely going on here.

"You're moving out, Kate?" Alec asked, sounding a little hurt and surprised. "What's the deal? Is it because I moved in? Because if it is—"

"It has nothing to do with you, Alec," Justin said sourly. "This is between Kate and me."

Kate and me? Okay, now Grace was sure there was something going on here. Too bad she had to drag the question of Bo into the middle of whatever it was.

"This has nothing to do with you," Kate said, facing Justin. She grabbed at a paper towel and wrapped it around her bleeding finger.

"Look," Justin said, his voice rising. "Don't take it out on Bo. That's not fair. You have a problem with me? Deal with me."

"Excuse me," Grace interjected, "but what are you two talking about?"

"It sounds juicy," Connor added, "but we'll need a bit of background to get all the nuances."

Kate ignored him and turned on Grace. "You don't know what we're talking about, *Racey*?"

"I told you, I don't think she does," Chelsea snapped.

"I definitely don't," Grace cried in frustration.

"Last summer," Kate said.

"Last summer," Grace repeated.

"'Thanks for another beautiful night. You're an amazing lover, but then you always have been. Signed Racey.' Does that ring a bell?"

Grace just stared at her. The words sounded familiar, only . . . Wait. Had she written a note like that to Justin?

And how would Kate know what that note had said? And why would she care?

Oh. *Oh.*

"You?" Grace asked slowly as the realization crept up on her. "You were the girl Justin was going out with last summer?"

All eyes swiveled to Kate. The kitchen was eerily quiet. The only noise was the steady hum of the two refrigerators and the bubbling of Alec's oatmeal.

"Going out, that's right," Kate replied at last. "And you were the girl he was sleeping with."

The eyes swiveled back to Grace and on to Justin, who was looking alternately furious and a little panic-stricken.

"Wow," Connor said to Justin in an awed tone. "I don't know whether to congratulate you or hand you a knife so you can protect yourself."

Kate? This was the girl that Justin had wept

over? This was his one great love? Kate, little miss sunshine and fresh air? Justin had never mentioned her name, never even said in so many words that she existed, but Grace had sensed some great hurt, that last time. She'd known there had been someone, but Kate?

Grace remembered the note now. For once she had lied to Justin. He hadn't been amazing. Not that last time. He'd been depressed and distracted. She'd left the note to reassure him.

"Well, well," Grace said softly. "I'm going to have to get up early more often. The things you can learn."

"I want your brother out of here," Kate snapped. She threw the uneaten melon in the trash and stormed out.

"As far as I'm concerned, he can stay," Chelsea said. "And unlike Kate, I'm staying here for the whole summer." Then she stormed out too.

Alec took his oatmeal and eased out the back door of the kitchen, obviously profoundly embarrassed.

"I'm going off to write for a while," Connor said. "I had been working on a poem, but now I'm thinking maybe I should try my hand at a stormy tale of young love."

Justin and Grace were alone in the kitchen. "You mad?" he asked softly.

Mad? No, not mad. "It would have been nice to know, I guess, but we're over, Justin. At least in that way." Grace stared out the window as a feeling washed over her—wistfulness, maybe, or regret? "In some other ways I don't feel like you and I will ever be truly over," she whispered.

"You're the best, Grace," Justin said gently.

Grace sighed. "Evidently not."

EIGHTEEN

"Hi. I'm Tina Taco."

"Yeah, right. And I'm Mayor McCheese."

"You want a coupon or not?"

"Let me ask you this—are you naked in there?"

Chelsea turned away. She was getting used to this kind of thing. This time the comment had come from a kid who looked about nine years old, the filthy-minded little creep.

Through the narrow grill she could see a world of people, all of whom seemed to be having a lot more fun than she was. Kids throwing a Frisbee over the heads of sleeping sunbathers; old people wading in the unusually calm water; a couple building an elaborate sand sculpture near the edge of the boardwalk.

Outside, the world was bright and smelled

fresh and clean. Inside her suit it was dark, and all Chelsea smelled was grease. She tried to convince herself it was the smell of Hawaiian Tropic and Bain de Soleil, but she knew it was just the aroma of the deep fryer, wafting out of Tina Wina Taco.

"Hi, would you like—"

"I'm in a hurry, all right? Bug somebody else."

Ah, yes. Working with the public was so rewarding. She hadn't been Tina Taco for long, and already she was having second thoughts. Aside from the obscene remarks and the rude comments, there were the little monsters who wanted to pull on her lettuce. She'd gone to Mass yesterday and listened to the priest's sermon about man's dual nature—the struggle between good and evil. Well, judging from her morning so far, evil was kicking good's butt.

"Hi, I'm Tina Taco, would you like a coupon?"

"Sure. Thanks." The young woman smiled sympathetically. "I spent a summer as a Teenage Mutant Ninja Turtle at an amusement park. I know what you're going through. Hang in there."

Finally. A friendly voice. Despite the ninety-degree heat, she'd been relieved she had to work today. At least she didn't have to spend the day tiptoeing through the minefield at home. She'd spent most of yesterday avoiding Kate and bickering with Greg.

"Hi, I'm Tina Taco, would you like a coupon?"

"Hey! Are you mild, spicy, or extra spicy?"

"Um, spicy?"

"Great. Why don't you let me take a bite?"

"Listen, explain something to me, you creep. Why would you come on to me? For all you know I'm really ugly inside here. I could have leprosy."

"I. . . I just thought it was funny."

"It wasn't." This was definitely getting old.

Chelsea spun around and headed up the boardwalk in the other direction. She hadn't gone far when she heard a familiar voice. "Oh, man. Is that *you,* Chelsea?"

Through the screen mesh, Chelsea could see Greg coming toward her.

"Chelsea, Chelsea. What do you think you're doing in that getup?"

"I'm working, Greg. You know, making my big five twenty-five an hour." She leaned closer. Greg looked horrified, embarrassed, and slightly nauseated. "Don't start, Greg," she warned. "I'm not up for another fight."

"I thought we finished this argument," Greg said firmly. "Chels, you don't need money this badly. This is humiliating. I mean, you're a taco!

You warned me, but still, seeing it in person . . ." He gave her a little nudge. "Come on, get out of that stupid getup. I want to hit the beach, and I want my babe by my side."

"I'm not off for another two hours."

"No, you're off right now," Greg ordered.

"Look, Greg, I know it's not much of a job, all right? But it was the only job I could find."

"I don't want to stand here all day arguing with you, Chelsea. I am not going to be seen talking to a giant taco, okay? You may not have any pride left, but I do."

Chelsea hesitated. She'd promised herself that she would be up-front, simply say what she wanted and then stick to it. She'd done it with Kate—at least in the end.

And what else was she going to do to earn money? She wasn't getting many hours with the Best Body job. And she had to pay the rent somehow. "Come on, Greg, I can't just walk out in the middle of my shift," she said at last, sounding more plaintive than she would have liked.

"Chels, I'm really starting to wonder about you," he said. "The Chelsea Lennox I know would not let herself be made into a clown. Thank God your father isn't here, or B.D. either. Your brother is on his way to becoming an officer and a gentleman, and you're the biggest fool on the beach."

216

The words struck Chelsea like a physical blow. Suddenly she pictured B.D. in his crisp midshipman's uniform, erect and proud. What if B.D. ever saw her this way, waddling down the boardwalk in full-dress taco? Greg was right. She was better than this. She *had* to be better than this.

"Now, let's get going."

Chelsea fingered her two-for-one coupons. She hated being forced to make decisions. Especially important decisions. And really, how good could her judgment be? She had ended up as a human taco.

"Chelsea. Now."

"Okay," Chelsea heard herself say. "Just let me get changed."

She didn't tell her boss what she was doing. He was busy in the kitchen anyway. Instead she just slipped off the costume, piling it in a corner of his tiny office. She scrawled a quick note and used a paperclip to hold it to a shred of Tina's lettuce. *Sorry, I have to quit. Family emergency.*

Outside, the relatively cool air felt good on her skin. Greg held out his arms invitingly and Chelsea let him wrap her up with them. He tilted her head back and leaned down to kiss her.

Whatever squabbles she'd ever had with Greg, his kisses, surprisingly sweet and tender for someone so forceful, had always made her forget them. His arms had always made her feel safe and secure. He had always made her feel beautiful, wanted, special.

Only, this time she felt none of those things.

"I said, how was your day?" Connor asked that afternoon.

"I'm sorry, did you ask me something?" Chelsea looked up from the black-and-white western she'd been staring at without the sound.

"Three times, actually. How was life in the big taco?"

"It stank," Chelsea said sullenly.

Connor nodded. "That's why they pay you, because it's unpleasant, eh? If it were fun, we'd have to pay them."

"I quit."

"You quit as Tina Taco?" Grace asked, stepping in from the kitchen. "You only had the job for like two days."

"Look, I don't need any more grief over it. Greg gave me plenty of that. Not to mention every pervert and weirdo on the boardwalk, which, by the way, is the home office of perverts and weirdos."

"I wasn't going to give you any grief," Grace said quietly.

"Nor I," Connor said. "I'm a man who makes

218

doughnuts. I'm not one to be looking down my nose."

Grace settled on the couch with the bad spring. "So I guess it's back to the job-hunting grind, huh? I could ask if they have any openings at The Claw, if you'd like."

"So long as it's a job with some dignity," Chelsea muttered. "Greg doesn't want me doing anything demeaning."

Grace and Connor exchanged a look. "*He* doesn't want you to do anything demeaning?" Grace echoed. "You mean Greg talked you into quitting?"

"No," Chelsea said quickly. "It wasn't that. I mean, face it. It was a stupid job." And yet, when she and Greg had passed by later that afternoon and noticed someone else dressed in the Tina Taco outfit, Chelsea had actually felt a strange twinge of jealousy. Which just went to show how truly dumb she was capable of being.

"It was a stupid job," Connor agreed. "No one will argue that. But undignified? Demeaning? Hey, you were earning an honest wage, weren't you?"

"My mother gave me that crap when I started waiting tables," Grace said angrily. "This line about how it was all beneath me."

Chelsea held up her hands. "Tina Taco is different. What if my family had ever seen me? You don't know my family. I mean, we're black, right?"

"You are?" Connor cried. "I wish someone had told me."

"The point is, see, in my family it's important to achieve something. My own great-great-grandfather was born a slave the year before the slaves were freed. When he died, he owned a hardware store. I know it doesn't sound like much, but he never even learned to read or write." Chelsea stopped, suddenly self-conscious. "Sorry. I've heard that story like a million times."

"My own family has stories like that too," Connor said. "And we probably tell them even more often. The Irish do love to talk. So go on."

"Okay, then there was my great-grandfather. He managed to attend Howard University and become a lawyer. My grandfather was one of the Tuskegee airmen—the first black fighter pilots. He shot down three German planes in World War Two. Then, of course, there's my dad. He's got a Ph.D. in economics and now he's this big consultant to politicians and corporations. And my mom publishes *Cityscape* magazine."

"Your family must be rich! What the hell are you doing working as a human taco?" Connor demanded. "Why aren't you sitting on your rear and showering all your friends with your charity?"

"Actually, we're not that rich." Chelsea laughed. "At least, I don't think we are. But my folks do expect me to live up to the standards of all my parents and grandparents and great-grandparents." She paused. "In short, not to be a fool on the boardwalk."

"You just got out of high school, Chelsea," Grace pointed out. "Don't you think you can wait a while before you become a war hero or a publisher?"

"Look at it this way," Connor said. "After being a taco, there's nowhere to go but up."

Chelsea stared at the TV screen. They didn't understand, but then, how could they? "The thing is," she said, "for a long time the only kinds of jobs black people could get were menial jobs. Maids. Busboys. Dishwashers. My folks are already having seizures because I'm majoring in art, which at least involves a college degree. Being a taco is just menial."

Connor sat forward and laced his fingers together. "Listen to me, Chelsea. There's no such thing as a menial job. A person does what he has to to hold body and soul together. Take my own family. My great-grandfather was poor, my grandfather was poor, and my father, too. Sad as it may seem, I make more money frying doughnuts here in America than my father ever made in his life. But my father lived and died a proud man, even though he never was more than a common laborer." Connor's expression softened. "He knew who he was, my father, and knew what he believed, no matter that he often seemed a silly bastard to me."

He sat back, and for a moment seemed lost in thought. Then he brightened, the old mischievous glint coming back. "Of course, he never resorted to being a human taco."

Chelsea snatched up a throw pillow and hurled it at him. "Well, I have to be off," he said, standing. "I've got doughnuts to fry and fill with goo." As he passed Chelsea, Connor touched her on the shoulder and gave her a little wink. Then, without a word, he bounded up the stairs, leaving Chelsea alone with Grace.

Grace smiled. "I think I kind of like that guy."

"Me too," Chelsea agreed, with more feeling than she'd intended.

"I guess it's a good thing at least some of the people in this house are talking." Grace stretched and yawned. "Anyway, you want my advice—don't ever let some guy push you into anything you don't want to do. No matter what, never let someone else make your decisions for you."

"Sounds like good advice," Chelsea said. "Thanks."

"It's free," Grace said. "And worth what you

paid for it. Besides, I should be the one thanking you, for standing up for Bo this morning."

"No big deal. He looks like an okay kid. Besides," Chelsea admitted a little sheepishly, "I was really just mad at Kate."

Grace headed toward her bedroom. "Are you going to work?" Chelsea asked.

"No, I'm off, which is no big loss. Mondays are not big money nights. I was just going back to my room to read for a while."

"Grace?" Chelsea said impulsively. "Listen, maybe you and I could hang together. Greg's off with his guy friends, and Kate's upstairs in seclusion, not talking to me really, not that I guess I want to talk to her, either. Maybe we could go see a movie or something."

"That won't help your relationship with Kate," Grace pointed out. "Not after what went down yesterday morning."

Grace was right. Kate would take it as a personal insult.

Chelsea shrugged philosophically. "Some wise person I know said I shouldn't let anyone else make my decisions for me," she said. "I guess maybe I can decide for myself who my friends are."

NINETEEN

The stick went twirling up and away, a dark blur against the enormous red sun. It landed in the water with a soft splash. Mooch raced to the end of the pier and took a flying leap, landing in a belly flop that sent gold-flecked spray into the air.

Kate watched from a chair near her bedroom window. With a sigh she tossed her pen and notepad aside. The letter to her parents wasn't going anywhere. Somehow, in a very short while, her life had changed so completely that writing about it seemed impossible.

Besides, it was too hot this evening to concentrate on much of anything. The air was strangely heavy and humid, so thick it was hard to breathe. Any hint of a breeze had vanished, leaving the bay flat and lifeless. Kate leaned forward in her chair. The back of her shirt might as well have been glued to her. She considered taking a shower, but in this oppressive heat, even that seemed like too much effort. It was easier just to sit here immobilized and stare out the window.

While Justin cheered him on, Mooch grabbed the stick in his teeth and began paddling back to the pier. He flopped his front paws up on the boards and hauled himself out of the water, dropping the stick at Justin's feet.

"Good boy, Mooch," Justin said, his voice just audible over the buzz of a boat's engine in the distance. "One more time? One more time? Okay, if you say so." He drew his arm back and let the stick fly.

With her bare foot, Kate traced a pattern in the sprinkling of sand on her hardwood floor. Weird stuff, sand. After a while, you got used to finding it everywhere. In the tub. In your hair. Between your sheets. One of these days she was going to have to break down and sweep out her room. On the other hand, why bother? She'd be out of here soon enough.

Out and alone.

After she'd gotten off work yesterday, Kate had spent most of the evening with Andrew, fruitlessly searching for a cheap efficiency apartment. Today, while they'd been cataloging slides, Andrew had actually made the gallant offer to let her temporarily move into his tiny cottage. She'd laughed it off, but now, hiding out in her room trying to avoid Justin, Grace, and Chelsea, it was almost starting to sound like a reasonable alternative.

It was just too hard to be around them now. Chelsea, who'd lied to her. Justin, who'd betrayed her. And Grace, who was a part of that betrayal.

At least when it had just been a note, before there was a face to attach to it, Kate had been able to pretend Racey was just another lifeguard groupie. But Grace? Grace was another story. Grace was smart and beautiful and couldn't be passed off as just another beach bimbo. It was too easy to see how Justin could be genuinely attracted to her.

"Mooch!"

Kate focused her gaze. Justin was standing at the end of the pier, waving frantically as a loud motor droned closer.

She leaned against the sill and then, in a flash she saw it—the speedboat cruising along, far too close to shore.

"Mooch!" Justin yelled. "Get back here! Come on boy, come on!"

But the dog was still happily paddling out into the bay, keeping his head just above the water as he made a beeline for the stick that floated just out of reach.

"Oh no," Kate whispered.

The boat's engine roared. A heavyset man stood at the wheel, grinning and oblivious.

"Mooch!" Justin cried.

The dog turned and looked, but too late. His head disappeared under the bow, and the boat sped on, leaving behind a wide, foaming wake.

Instantly Justin dove off the pier. Without thinking, Kate jumped from her seat and raced for the stairs.

She ran across the lawn to the pier, just in time to see Justin surface, gulp in a lungful of air, and take another deep dive. He seemed to be underwater forever. Then, in an explosion of spray, he surfaced twenty yards away. He was holding something in his right hand.

"Please let him be all right," Kate prayed.

With a few strong strokes, Justin reached the end of the pier. Gently he lifted Mooch's limp body onto it.

"Oh, God, Justin," Kate cried. "Is he okay?"

Justin propelled himself up onto the pier and knelt beside Mooch. "He's breathing, but look at his head. Look at his poor head."

Kate knelt beside him. Blood pooled beneath Mooch's head. One ear was barely attached, and the gruesome white of shattered bone poked through the wound.

"I'll get my keys," Kate said.

She sprinted back to the house and grabbed her purse and a towel. When she came out, Justin was already sitting in the front seat, talking steadily to Mooch as he cradled the big dog in his arms.

"Here," she said, passing the towel to Justin. "Try to stop the bleeding."

The drive to the animal hospital seemed to drag on forever. "He'll be okay, Justin," Kate said, trying to give him a reassuring smile. But a glance at the blood-soaked towel in his hand made her wonder if Mooch wasn't already dead.

When they finally reached the animal hospital, Kate jerked the car to a stop in front of the little one-story building and ran around the side to open the door for Justin.

Justin looked at her. "He's stopped breathing."

"Let's get him inside," Kate said firmly.

As soon as they were in the door, two white-coated vet assistants hustled Mooch back to an operating room. Kate and Justin sat on orange plastic chairs in the waiting room. She took care of filling out the necessary forms, while Justin sat motionless, chin resting in his hand, eyes fixed ahead. He was shirtless, and his shorts were covered in blood. In the chill air-conditioned room, she could tell he was shivering.

Kate handed the forms to a receptionist. "She said they won't know for a while yet," Kate said when she returned to her seat. When he didn't answer, she said, "You must be freezing, Justin."

He shrugged. "Sorry I, uh, you know. You know, got upset."

"Justin, it's okay to be upset."

"See, it's just that Mooch is—" His voice choked with emotion. He tried again to say something and failed.

"He's a tough dog, Justin." She laid her hand on his shoulder for a moment.

"Yeah. He's a tough old dog."

For a while, the silence settled in again. Other patients came and went—a cat whose tail had gotten slammed in a door, a German shepherd running a high fever, a motherless newborn kitten.

Justin sighed and took a deep breath, then sat up straight. "Man, I'm sorry. I'm acting like a wimp."

"No, you're acting like a guy who loves his dog," Kate said.

"Well, stuff happens, doesn't it?" Justin said, his voice flat and emotionless. "You get over it and get on with your life. Dogs don't live forever. Mooch has been my dog for, I don't know, since I was nine. I got him right after my dad walked out.

He just wandered by one day, hungry, looking to bum some food. My dad never wanted me to have a dog. He thought they were trouble, I guess."

Kate frowned. Had she heard Justin right? "Justin, I always assumed from the way you talked about him that your father had passed away."

Justin shook his head. "No. Might as well have, but as far as I know, he's not dead."

"You're saying he left you and your mother?"

"It's old news. He bailed out. We got over it. That's life. Stuff happens, you deal with it."

"And you got Mooch right after that?"

"Yeah. I know, it's pathetic isn't it?" he said with a trace of self-mockery. "Lonely little kid gets a mutt instead of a father. There ought to be violins playing. Maybe I could tell my sad story on the Oprah Winfrey show."

Kate looked away. "And you've never heard from him since?" she asked softly.

"No. My mother eventually got a divorce. When the husband isn't there for a few years, it's pretty easy to arrange. You remember she was going out with that guy Norman last summer? I told you about him. He's all right. He loves her, and he was always cool to me. After they married, he got transferred to some hick town in Vermont. They asked me to come along, but, hey, Vermont? There's no ocean in Vermont."

"I'm glad she's happy," Kate said. "Your mom, I mean."

"Hmm. Me too. She deserves a break."

The cat with the broken tail emerged from the back, sporting a splint and a sour expression. Justin caught the eye of the vet assistant, but she just shook her head regretfully and gave him a little smile.

Justin swallowed and looked straight ahead. He gave a small nod, as if he were resigning himself to the inevitable.

Impulsively Kate reached for his hand. He didn't look at her, didn't even acknowledge her, really, except for the fingers that tightened around her own.

"You know, that's why Grace and I got together," he said suddenly.

Kate froze. Why would he tell her about this? And did she really want to know?

"We were the two most screwed-up people in high school, I think." He made a sardonic face. "Her folks were a real pair. Her mom is this cold bitch, a real ice queen except when she's drunk. Her dad was useless. I guess it was ninth or tenth grade when they finally got divorced. Grace got kind of wild for a while. Me, I was already wild." He smiled crookedly. "We were wild together."

Kate bit her lip. She didn't really want to hear about Justin and Grace helping each other through their pain. It made it all seem too understandable, too forgivable. She wanted it all in simple black and white, not shades of gray.

"Anyway, that lasted about a year. We both just got over it. She went her way and I went mine. I think we both knew if we stayed together, we'd only drag each other down. And I was tired of being down." He stopped talking and looked into Kate's eyes. "That's when I met you."

"Mr. Garrett?"

It was the assistant. Her face was unreadable. Relieved? Sad? Perhaps she'd had to give too many pet owners bad news to let her own feelings show.

"Yes?" Justin said.

"The doctor will be right out."

"Can you tell us—" Kate began, but the assistant had already disappeared.

"He didn't make it," Justin said softly.

"You don't know that," Kate said. She squeezed his hand a little tighter. "Wait for the doctor."

It took several long minutes for the door to open. A middle-aged woman in a white lab coat came out.

"That old mutt of yours has one hard head," she said.

"He's alive?" Justin asked in a whisper.

"Of course he's alive." The vet grinned broadly. "I'm the best vet within a hundred miles. You think I'd let him die? Now, he's going to need to stay with us for a while so we can keep him on antibiotics, but I think he'll be all right in a week or so. I'll give you a call."

Justin stood, his hand slipping from Kate's grasp. "Thanks, Doc," he said, reaching over to shake the vet's hand.

He spun around and headed for the door, but not so quickly that Kate didn't see the tears streaming down his face.

By the time Kate got to the car, Justin was already sitting in the passenger's seat, calm and back in control. The air was still stifling, but a light drizzle had begun to fall, so they raised the top.

"Listen, Kate," Justin said as she put the car in gear.

"Yes?"

"Thanks. For driving me here, and for staying." He looked over at her. "And for running that red light on the way over."

"I ran a red light?"

"Two, actually."

Kate waited. She wanted him to finish what he'd started to tell her in the waiting room. Was

233

she just another girl to fill the space on the rebound from Grace? Had he really meant it when he'd told Kate he loved her?

But Justin said nothing more.

"Sure, Justin," Kate said softly. "Any time."

TWENTY

"Order anything you want, big guy. I'm buying."

Chelsea laid the tattered, greasy menu in front of Greg and settled back on the straight-backed wooden booth. One of the charms of Floaters was that not only was the service lousy, the tables and booths were small and uncomfortable. But it opened directly onto the boardwalk and was a great place to sit and people-watch, especially when the lunch rush was still two hours away. The boardwalk crowd passed by like some not very interesting movie, acted by a cross-section of sunburned, grumpy, giddy, poorly dressed, vacationing humanity.

At the same time, to passersby, the inside of Floaters looked more like some darkened cave than a restaurant. A cave populated by faces that turned subtly hostile whenever a tourist trespassed on this private domain. Not that the tourists were really missing much. The burgers, however, were great, and the restaurant was always filled with lifeguards, cops, and other locals who worked along the boardwalk.

"You're buying?" Greg asked. "You seem to have forgotten, you're unemployed."

"Not anymore," Chelsea said happily. "Can you believe it? Mr. McMurdo is putting me on full-time. I started working with him yesterday and we got along really well. The other girl who was working for him quit to have a baby, so he's going to let me take care of all the sign-ups for this Best Bod, and then the *next* contest, I'll organize the whole thing. He says he has too much other stuff going on to mess with it himself. In fact, I have to get down there by ten thirty, so don't order anything that takes too long to cook."

The look on Greg's face was easy to read. He was disappointed and making no effort to hide it. "'Best Bod'? What kind of a job is that?"

"I told you before, it's a contest," Chelsea explained. "They hold them all the time, and there are prizes for the best-looking girl in a bikini and the best-looking guy in a bathing suit."

Greg just stared at her.

"The pay is better than Tina Taco," Chelsea

said defensively. "I'm getting six bucks an hour."

"Chelsea, I don't—"

"Hey, kids," someone called.

Chelsea looked up. Alec was approaching their table. She saw Justin wave from across the room, where he and an older lifeguard were settling into a booth.

"Hi, Alec. Any more word on Mooch?"

"Justin called the vet first thing this morning. Mooch is doing great."

"I'm so glad. He's the only one who really liked my meatballs."

"We're just finishing up a combination late breakfast and very early lunch over there that makes me long for your meatballs," Alec said. "We're expecting a big crowd this afternoon, so we may not be getting a lunch break later. It's eat now or starve later." He smiled and shrugged his shoulders. "So, you get a new job yet?"

"Maybe." Chelsea glanced guiltily at Greg. "I'm not totally sure."

"Well, hang in there. Sooner or later somebody will fall for that smile of yours. See you. Later, Greg." Alec rejoined Justin and the other lifeguard at their table.

"Is that what happened, Chels?" Greg demanded. "Your new boss fall for that big smile of yours?"

"Greg, that's not the way it is."

"What *is* the way it is, Chelsea?" He glanced over at Alec and Justin and sighed. "What are you doing here in Ocean City, living with that bunch of losers, anyway?"

"What are you talking about?" Chelsea cried. "Kate's been my best friend for years, and she's not a loser."

Greg held up a hand. "No, you're right. I stand corrected. *Kate* is not a loser. She's a girl who's going someplace. But how about that waitress? Or the Irish guy who couldn't make it in his own country? Or your two lifeguards over there, Tweedledum and Tweedledumber?"

Chelsea recoiled at the sudden venom in Greg's voice. She stared at him, right into his eyes. He was still talking, leaning forward to make his points, but Chelsea was no longer listening. She was just watching the expressions, watching the way he leaned toward her, put his hands across the table, dominated the space.

"Are you listening to me?" Greg demanded.

Chelsea didn't answer, which just made Greg angrier. "I said, are you listening to—"

"Her name is Grace."

Greg looked perplexed. "What?"

"The waitress, as you called her. Her name is Grace, and she's my friend."

"That girl is not your friend."

"Yes, she is," Chelsea said, her voice growing firmer. "And as for Justin and Alec, hey, I don't know either one all that well, but Kate says Justin's smart and fun and interesting and Kate has good taste. As for Connor"—Chelsea fought to control her growing anger—"as for Connor, Greg, I think he's more of a man than you'll ever be."

Greg's eyes blazed. It was an expression she had seen before and she knew that it was time to give way to him. To let him have his way for now, then slowly, over time, turn him around.

Only she wasn't going to do that, not this time.

"You and that Irish guy," Greg said in a dangerously soft voice. "I must admit, I'm surprised. I would have thought if you were going after white guys, you'd go for your boy Alec over there."

"Greg, shut up."

"What? What did you just say to me?"

If Greg was surprised, so was she. "I said shut up. Furthermore, get out of my life. Don't call me, don't write me, don't even think about me. This is *my* life. And I'll pick my own friends, and I'll choose my own jobs, and if you don't like it, you can go to hell."

Go to hell? Had she really just said that?

Greg's jaw dropped open, a fact Chelsea

found incredibly funny. A slow smile spread across her face. Was this how Kate felt all the time? Just right out front like this?

Greg was looking a little uncertain. "Come on home with me," he said, lowering his voice. "I'm leaving tomorrow, Chelsea, and we'll have plenty of time to talk this over when we get back."

"Leave, Greg. Go away." This was all right. She could get into this assertive thing. In fact, when she was done with Greg, she was going to assert herself at someone else.

Greg stood up. "If I walk out of here, I'm never coming back."

"I'll hold you to that." Chelsea pointed. "Get out."

"I'm serious."

"Get out."

"I'll count to three . . ."

"Greg?"

"What?"

Chelsea grinned. "Bye."

He hesitated, then, with a last angry glare, stalked out of the restaurant.

For a long time Chelsea just stared at the empty place where he had been. It would be all right to cry now, but somehow no tears came. Greg was out of her life. He'd been her boyfriend longer than any guy she'd ever dated.

And all she felt was numb, and a little giddy.

Something appeared on her table, as if by magic. "I didn't order a hot-fudge sundae," Chelsea objected.

"I know," the waitress said. "It is a little early for ice cream, but I'm supposed to tell you it's compliments of Tweedledum and Tweedledumber, and they want to know which of them is which."

"Hey. Those are *my* cookies. You could try asking first." Kate sagged against the sink and poured herself a desperately needed glass of water. She'd just gone for a five-mile run along the bay. The first running she'd done since coming to Ocean City.

Bo looked up from his perch on the counter and insolently popped another Nilla Wafer into his mouth. "They're not very good. They're, like, the most boring cookie you can buy."

"Sorry to disappoint you," Kate said dryly. "What kind do you like?"

"Oreos," he said, showing no sign he'd detected her sarcasm. "I thought you'd be at work by now. Everyone else is gone, except Connor. He's up in his room. Grace got called in to do a lunch shift." Bo grinned and dug into the cookie box.

"My boss had to go to a seminar this morning, so I have the morning off," Kate said. "Look, Bo,

241

as long as you're here, the very least you can do is live by the rules. It's not like we have a lot of them."

"Rules, huh? That's why I moved out on my mom. Too many stupid rules."

"This isn't a stupid rule," Kate said reasonably. "This is about the fact that those are mine. I bought them so that *I* could eat them. You want to eat something, your sister has her own shelf in the pantry and her own section of the refrigerator."

"I checked. She didn't have any cookies. Actually, she didn't have anything except for a six-pack of beer." Bo looked Kate right in the eye and dug out another cookie, crunching it noisily. "Is that against the rules too?"

Kate felt a sudden, surprising burst of anger. *You're overreacting,* she told herself. But somehow she couldn't seem to look at Bo without seeing Grace. And she couldn't think of Grace without getting angry at Justin all over again.

"I know you don't want me here," Bo said.

"Who told you that?" Kate asked.

"Gracie." He smiled slyly. "I know what your problem is."

"I don't have a problem." *Don't let him bait you,* Kate instructed herself. *He's looking for a fight. You're the adult—more or less. You're the one who has to stay rational.*

"Sure you do," Bo said. "His name's Justin. What do you think I am, stupid? You want him, but Grace is the one who's had him. And she can have him again, any time she wants."

So much for staying rational. "You . . . you little," Kate cried, clenching her fists. "You little jerk."

"Hey, you don't scare me," Bo said. "I've handled a lot worse than you could ever throw at me."

"Is that what Grace told you? Huh? That she could have Justin any time she wanted? Fine, you're right. I guess if she's ready to hop into bed with him whenever he wants, she can have him."

The instant the words were out of her mouth, Kate knew she'd gone too far.

"Don't you say that about Grace," Bo warned, stepping toward her. "You take it back."

"You're the one who started this fight."

"I did not," Bo said.

"Did too," Kate answered automatically. *Wonderful. This was really mature.*

"Did *not.*"

The doorbell rang. Well, let it ring. Someone would get it. She was in the middle of descending to the level of a fifteen-year-old—something she hadn't done even when she *was* fifteen.

The doorbell rang again. No, no one else was awake.

Kate tore her gaze away from Bo and stalked into the living room. She yanked open the front door. "What?" she demanded.

"Hello, I'm Mrs. Caywood."

It took several seconds for Kate to register the name and the face. Grace's mother. Bo's mother.

"I'm Kate Quinn. What can I do for you? Grace isn't here right now."

Mrs. Caywood looked sharply at Kate. "I know. She's at work. I checked ahead of time."

"Then—" Kate began.

"May I come in?"

It seemed like a reasonable request, but somehow Kate didn't like the tone. It didn't sound like a request. It sounded more like a threat.

"First tell me how I can help you," Kate said. Without really meaning to, she blocked the doorway.

"Fine." Mrs. Caywood managed an icy smile. "I'd like to pick up my son, Bo, and take him home with me."

"Bo?" Kate repeated.

"Bo. My fifteen-year-old son, Bo, who should be home with his mother."

Kate took a deep breath.

"I kind of think you should talk to Grace

244

about this, Mrs. Caywood," Kate said.

Mrs. Caywood's eyes went colder still. "Look, dear. Bo is my son. He's my responsibility. Not yours, and not Grace's. So just stand aside and let me go in and get him."

"He's not here."

"Yes he is, and I'm going in to get him." Mrs. Caywood took a step forward, but Kate didn't budge.

"This is my house, Mrs. Caywood. You can't just barge in." Kate had wanted to say *He's in the kitchen, help yourself,* but something had held her back.

"Please get out of my way," Mrs. Caywood demanded. She put her hand on Kate's shoulder and shoved.

Kate resisted, and with the back of her hand knocked the older woman's arm away. "I'll call the police and have you arrested if you touch me again," Kate said firmly, to keep a tremor out of her voice. "This is *my* house. Mine and my roommates'." She tried to swallow, but her dry mouth wasn't cooperating.

For a moment Mrs. Caywood just glared at her. Then she spun around and stormed down the steps to her Mercedes.

Kate closed the door with trembling fingers. As an afterthought, she turned the lock. She made it as far as the couch and slumped down, closing her eyes.

When she opened her eyes, she saw Bo standing over her. "Great," she muttered. "What do *you* want? More cookies? Help yourself."

"Why did you do that?" Bo asked.

Kate sighed wearily. "Do what?"

"Why'd you lie? Why didn't you give me up? You obviously don't like me."

Kate shook her head slowly. Why? Good question. "I don't know, to be honest with you. I don't like you. I think you're a brat. I don't much like your sister, either. But I also don't like people telling me what to do."

Bo narrowed his eyes. "She can make trouble for you, you know. My mom knows everyone, and she has a lot of money."

Kate laughed softly. "Well, everything else has gone wrong since I got here. Why should today be any different?"

"Not many people have ever stood up to my mom," Bo said.

"She is rather forceful."

"So are you. Thanks. I owe you one." Bo dropped onto the couch.

"I'm still hungry," Kate said. She stood up, grabbed Bo by the hand and pulled him up as well. "Come on down to the boardwalk with me.

If I hurry, I have time before I have to get to work. I'll buy you a cookie."

"I'm still on Gracie's side," Bo warned.

"Yeah, and you're still a pain," Kate said. "Let's go."

TWENTY-ONE

"Is this, like, where I sign up for the Best Body on the Beach contest?"

Chelsea smiled up at the girl. It was funny how many people asked that question, despite the fact that there was a sign on the table that read BEST BODY SIGN-UP and a big yellow and blue BEST BODY ON THE BEACH banner on the wall. But then, the four people she'd signed up so far, guys and girls, hadn't been geniuses.

"Yes, it is," Chelsea answered. "There's a seventy-five-dollar entry fee."

"So, like, I have to give you seventy-five dollars?"

"Like, yes." The large fee seemed to discourage most people from entering.

"And what's the prize?" the girl asked. "I mean, like, what do I win?"

"Well, the first-place prize for women entrants is five hundred dollars," Chelsea said. "Plus two free nights at this hotel and dinner for two at Seafood Sally's." The hotel was the Ocean City Grand, a fancy fifteen-story hotel at the northern end of the boardwalk. The contest was going to be held right outside on the beach, and the hotel was allowing Mr. McMurdo, Chelsea's boss, to use this little corner of the lobby to sign up contestants.

"Rad," the girl said. "But I have to ask you something." She lowered her voice to a confidential whisper. "There isn't any rule that you have to be all natural, is there?"

"What do you mean?" Chelsea asked.

"I mean, you know, if your boobs have been kind of improved."

Don't look at her chest. You looked at her chest.

"No. At least, no one told me there was," Chelsea said, trying very hard not to stare. "Are they—?"

"Oh, sure. I went from thirty-four A to thirty-six C."

"Really."

"They look great now," the girl assured Chelsea.

"I'll take your word for it," Chelsea said quickly.

"They're my strong point."

"Points," Chelsea corrected.

Okay, Chelsea thought as the girl walked away, *this is a pretty dumb job.* But at least it wasn't quite as dumb as her stint as Tina Taco. It did pay seventy-five cents an hour more, and the air-conditioned hotel lobby was a lot more pleasant than the taco suit. Air-conditioning was a big plus. So was sitting in her nice, comfortable chair instead of walking the boards.

"Hey, is this the place to sign up for the Best Bod contest?"

Chelsea was ready to offer a mildly sarcastic response when she took a closer look at the source of the question. She had to crane her neck back to see all of him. She felt her jaw drop open, and didn't even care.

It took several tries before she regained the use of her voice. "Yes, this is the place."

He grinned a huge, winning smile.

Funny, but every lingering memory of Greg's face had just evaporated. And they'd been broken up for only a day.

You are beautiful, Chelsea thought. *I don't even care if you are a complete idiot. I will gladly bear your children.*

"Excellent," he said. "Are you going to compete too?"

"Me? Oh, no."

"Why not?" the man asked. "You look like you could hold your own."

Chelsea saw his dark eyes travel over her body. Perhaps he would like a closer look? Say, in his room? In his car? Right here on the lobby floor?

"Here," she finally said. "You have to fill out this form. Also, it costs seventy-five dollars. But if you don't have the money, I could probably—"

"No problem. Is it the same price for women?"

"Yes," Chelsea said.

"Great. I'll sign up for my wife, too."

"Wife?"

"Shawnelle Scott. Maybe you've heard of her. She took second place in the national aerobics championship."

So he was married. So he was married to some fitness nut who could probably bounce quarters off her hard butt. So—

So she'd better get on with her job and stop dreaming.

"See you at the contest, Mr. Scott," she said.

"In the winner's circle," he said confidently.

Good-bye. I will always love you. Someday, somehow, after you grow tired of your wife and you want someone with a sense of humor and very little muscle tone—

"Hi."

It was Kate. Chelsea's first instinct was to be embarrassed. Mostly because she knew Kate disapproved of her latest career move. But also because she had been busy watching the retreating buns of the perfect Mr. Scott.

"Hi, Kate," Chelsea said guardedly.

"So, this is where you work. I, uh, I just thought I'd come down and say hi. I got my work done early. Shelby said I should go out and get a tan."

Chelsea looked at her friend. Unofficially they weren't speaking. Unofficially they were as broken up as Chelsea and Greg.

"Can you take a break?" Kate asked almost shyly.

"I guess so." Chelsea made sure the checks and money she'd collected were safely in her pocket, then followed Kate outside onto the boardwalk.

"I guess you heard that Mooch got hurt," Kate said.

"Alec told me," Chelsea confirmed.

"I went with Justin to the vet hospital. We talked. And afterward, I realized I needed someone else to talk to. And I didn't have anyone."

Chelsea nodded. "I guess I felt the same

about breaking up with Greg."

"You didn't!" Kate grabbed her arm. "You actually broke up with Greg?" she cried.

"Yeah, yesterday. Finally, huh? I was unbelievably assertive. Like you'd be if you drank a lot of coffee."

Kate smiled. "I'm glad, Chelsea, really glad. But how do you feel?"

"I'm glad too." She paused. "I think. Ask me again later after it sinks in."

"Greg was never right for you. He was always trying to make decisions for you, without even asking what you wanted." Kate gazed off toward the water. "I hate people like that. Even though sometimes I *am* people like that."

"It's my own fault. I should learn to stand up for what I want. And I'm starting to now. At least with Greg." Chelsea followed Kate's line of vision out to the gentle sea. "I'll try to be more up-front with you, too. So I'm still staying in our house." She fell silent for a moment. "But I don't want you to get lost. You're my best friend in the whole world and I'm really sorry I didn't tell you about Grace. And it just about killed me not being able to tell you about Greg last night. It's like it didn't really happen until I told you about it. So forgive me, all right, because I can't stand not having you as my best friend."

Kate hung her head. "Tell me about it. We're going out to tag sharks this afternoon and I realized how much I was looking forward to telling you about it and then . . ." She brushed away a tear. Then both girls laughed.

"Do you think it would look too weird if we hugged here in the middle of the boardwalk?" Kate asked.

"You have to be a lot weirder than that to look weird on the boardwalk," Chelsea said, giving her friend a long hug. "I promise never to hide anything from you again," she said. "And I'll never try to manipulate you again."

"And I promise I won't be bossy and try to tell you what to do."

"Yeah, right," Chelsea said.

Kate grinned. "Okay, how about this? We both just be our usual selves. Only we swear, no matter how mad we are, that we'll always, always talk to each other. I can deal with hating your guts. I just can't deal with not being able to tell you stuff."

"That's a deal," Chelsea said solemnly. "And tonight, as soon as we both get home from work, we lock ourselves in my room and tell all."

"I'll be there," Kate promised.

TWENTY-TWO

"He's huge!" Kate said that afternoon as she stared down at the gray-blue monster that lurked just below the surface of the water.

The shark lolled onto its side and seemed to stare at her with a hideous, accusing eye. A hook, attached to a strong line, dangled from his mouth. He was lying in a loose canvas sleeve attached to a winch. The sleeve restricted his movements somewhat, although not enough to satisfy Kate.

The boat rolled in a large swell, and Kate grabbed for the railing, convinced she was headed right into the gaping jaws of the shark. A strong arm caught her around the waist and held her tightly until the boat righted itself.

Andrew to the rescue. "Thanks," Kate gasped.

Andrew released her and wagged a scolding

finger. "Always watch your balance. You fall over, and we might not get you back in time."

Kate glanced down again at the hammerhead shark. Instead of the usual streamlined snout, a hammerhead had fleshy protrusions on either side of its head where its eyes were located. No way around it, these guys were ugly.

"Do they eat people?" she asked nervously. So far she'd been a model of scientific detachment at work. But that had been in the lab. The nice, safe lab where the sharks were kept in nice, safe tanks.

"Well, they can be dangerous," Andrew said. "You know the creature from the *Alien* movies? The perfect killing machine? Sharks are the closest thing you'll see to that on planet Earth."

"Aside from human beings," Shelby interjected as she came up behind them. "You two ready?"

Andrew nodded, and Kate did her best not to look terrified. Carefully Shelby climbed down a rope ladder onto a latticelike wood platform that rested just inches above the shark. Andrew followed her.

"Your turn," he called to Kate.

Easy for him to say. Kate made it down the ladder, despite the fact that her knees had turned to liquid. As soon as she settled on the platform, the boat caught a small wave and water rushed up around her ankles, lifting the shark as well.

"Don't sweat it," Andrew said calmly as he handed her the tagging stick, a long pole with a stainless-steel needle on the end.

While Kate clutched at the support ropes, Shelby shoved a long syringe into the shark and withdrew blood.

"He's all yours, Kate," Andrew said.

Kate knelt on the platform and positioned the tagging stick the way Andrew had shown her. She applied pressure, puncturing the shark's sandpaper skin. Then she withdrew the stick, leaving behind a brightly colored steel and plastic tag.

The work was supposed to be done quickly to minimize the stress on the shark, and Kate was relieved when Andrew cut the heavy fishing line that held the hammerhead and they were all able to clamber back aboard.

"Now anyone who catches this shark, anywhere in the world, will call us up and let us know where the guy turned up and how much he weighed," Shelby explained.

"And people actually do this?" Kate asked.

"Sure. We get great cooperation from fishermen. Without them, we wouldn't have much of a program."

Over the course of the afternoon, they hauled up and tagged four more sharks—three white-tipped, and a young great white. Kate's fear didn't go away, but the work was exhilarating. It was something she had never done before—been intensely afraid and still overcome the fear.

Unless, of course, you counted her run-in with Mrs. Caywood.

Kate stood in the bow on the way back in, letting the cold spray rinse her clean. In the distance O.C. glittered in the low rays of the afternoon sun, looking just as magical as it had the day she and Chelsea had first driven into town. But somehow, out here on the sea, the town seemed small and irrelevant. The city and its people and their problems were nothing to this great ocean.

Was this how Justin felt about the sea? Was this why he set his sights on leaving the land behind? Maybe he thought that out here, his problems would seem smaller, that missing fathers and failed romances and all the pains of every-day life would hurt less.

"Hey, gorgeous." Kate turned to see Andrew on the flying bridge.

She smiled up at him and reminded herself again how lucky she was. Andrew was a great guy. He was smart, he was handsome, he was idealistic, and he was great on the dance floor. Not only that, he could cook. At least he *claimed* he could. He'd volunteered to make her dinner tomorrow night, after work.

They made a great pair, she and Andrew. He was the kind of guy she'd always dreamed of. Even her parents would approve.

They pulled up to the Safe Seas pier. Kate hopped off to catch the rope and loop it over the piling, securing the bow.

Halfway down the pier as she headed back to the Safe Seas office, Kate stopped dead. A small blue sports car was waiting at the end, top down.

"Hi," Grace said as she climbed out. She was dressed in her waitress uniform.

Kate stared at her doubtfully. "Hi."

"I've been waiting. I called the office and they told me when you'd be getting back. Don't worry—I won't take up much of your time." She gestured at her uniform. "I just have a little while before I have to be at work."

Kate nodded and crossed her arms over her chest.

Grace removed her sunglasses and locked eyes with Kate. "Bo was asleep by the time I got home last night, but this morning he told me what happened. Why did you stand up for him? I thought you'd jump at the chance to get rid of Bo."

Kate nodded. "I thought I would too."

"Then why?"

Kate's first impulse was to toss off some glib reply, or tell Grace it was really none of her business. But it was clear from Grace's expression that she wanted a real answer. "Your mother tried to intimidate me," she said at last.

"And you don't like being intimidated," Grace remarked with just a trace of mockery.

"I guess that's right," Kate said evenly. "I guess I don't."

"It's the same reason you don't like me. I intimidate you." It was a statement of fact, not a challenge or an accusation.

"I suppose you do, a little," Kate admitted. "You're . . . never mind."

"No, go ahead. A little honesty never hurt anyone," Grace said. "Much."

Kate shrugged. "I guess you seem more experienced. More sophisticated in some ways. You drink. You . . . you know."

"Have sex?" Grace offered.

Kate felt a flicker of a smile. "It's not just that."

For a moment both girls were silent. Then Grace laughed. "So, you think I'm a hard, immoral slut. And I think you're a prissy suburban ice princess. How are we going to live together?"

"We're not," Kate said flatly. "I'm looking for another place."

"I know," Grace said, her voice subdued. "It complicates your life having Justin around. It complicates it a lot more having me around while Justin's around. And I could probably set your mind at ease on that score, but I don't like to make promises unless I'm absolutely sure I can keep them. Still—" She looked past Kate to some distant place on the water. "I do wish you'd stay."

"But I must complicate your life too, Grace."

"Sure you do." Grace grinned. "But it's the complications that make life interesting, Kate. And there's nothing I hate worse than boredom." Suddenly she was serious again. "Besides, you stood up for Bo. And that's something I won't forget."

"It was no big deal."

"Just the same, thanks."

Grace turned away and headed back toward her car. She climbed in, started the engine, and with a casual wave, drove away, kicking up a cloud of dust.

Kate shook her head, watching her disappear.

"Who was that?" Shelby asked as she came walking down the pier.

"That was either my housemate or one of

261

your sharks," Kate replied. "I'm not entirely sure which."

"You don't have to walk me up," Kate told Andrew as he pulled his car in front of her house after dinner the next night. "This seems like a pretty safe neighborhood."

"Are you afraid I'll try to kiss you good night at your front door?" Andrew joked.

Kate leaned over and kissed him lightly on the lips. "I'd be pretty insulted if you didn't," she said. "I just didn't want to make you get out of your car. It is pretty late."

Well, that was at least partly true. It was late. But she also didn't want to put on a show on the front porch for her housemates. She could do without anyone critiquing her performance. Not to mention the possibility that Alec or Connor might happen by. Alec would just be embarrassed, and Connor . . . well, you never knew what he might have to say.

Then, of course, there was Justin.

No, she scolded herself angrily. She was not about to let Justin's presence on the scene interfere with her love life.

"On second thought," Kate said, smiling, "I guess there could be boogie men lurking in the bushes."

262

They walked slowly toward the porch. "Beautiful night," Andrew commented, pausing to gaze up at the stars.

"It was a beautiful night," Kate agreed. She slipped her arms around his broad shoulders. "Thanks to you."

It had been, too. They'd started the evening by driving up to the nature preserve to watch the sun go down over the peaceful salt marshes. Afterward Andrew had cooked a wonderful dinner at his cottage, complete with candles and a red-checked tablecloth. As a joke he'd rented a video of *Jaws,* but they'd never quite gotten around to watching it.

They'd ended up on the ancient pullout couch that doubled as his bed, where they'd spent the next couple hours kissing, touching, getting to know each other, kissing some more. It had felt a little strange, maybe because she was a little out of practice. After Justin, her senior year had been more or less a dating wasteland. Andrew was the first guy she'd felt this way about in a long time.

Still, there hadn't been any major fireworks tonight. That was normal, wasn't it? She and Andrew were still in the getting-to-know-you phase.

They stopped at the foot of the steps. "Let's

not go up on the porch," Kate suggested. "Those steps creak so loudly they'll wake up anyone who's asleep—which I'm hoping everyone is."

Andrew drew her closer. He really did have a great jawline. Great smile. Great eyes.

"I had a fantastic night," Andrew said softly. "I don't remember when I've enjoyed being with someone more."

"I had a great night too," Kate responded, but somehow when she said it, it sounded a little lame.

She could tell that Andrew was about to kiss her. She'd noticed that he always started by tilting his head to the left, then closing his eyes. Odd, her noticing details like that.

Right on schedule he kissed her, and she kissed him back, a long, deep kiss that left her breathless. No fireworks, but a few sparks.

"I guess I have to say good night," he said softly, leaning his forehead against hers and gazing into her eyes.

"Night," she said. She kissed him again, this time lightly on the lips. "It was great."

"It was," he agreed. Reluctantly he released her, and with a small wave, headed back to his car and drove off.

Kate watched him go, then glanced up at the house. Chelsea's window was dark. Too bad. She needed to talk to someone about Andrew, to help her get her feelings sorted out. Maybe she'd wake Chelsea up. Chels wouldn't mind, as long as the topic was guys. But no. Chelsea had to get up early tomorrow for the Best Body contest. She'd need all the sleep she could get.

Kate heard a noise, a soft footfall. She turned and saw Justin in the shadows.

"Sorry," he said. "I wasn't trying to eavesdrop. I raided the kitchen and was on my way back to the boathouse." He held up a bag of potato chips. Evidence.

How much had he seen? she wondered, half angry, half embarrassed. "You could have told me you were lurking there in the dark."

Justin nodded. "I guess I could have." He stepped closer. "He seems like a nice guy."

"He is."

Justin nodded again and moved even closer. Some part of Kate's brain told her to walk away, head upstairs, retreat. But she didn't want to give Justin the satisfaction. She wasn't concerned about him. He had no effect on her. None.

"I only want to know one thing," Justin whispered. He tossed aside the potato chips.

"What do you want to know?" Kate asked in a voice that betrayed her by quavering.

In one fluid motion Justin took her in his arms and kissed her.

It might have lasted a moment. It might have lasted a year. She couldn't say. And as for which way he tilted his head, or when he closed his eyes—well, she had better things to do than think.

Justin slowly pulled away. "I just want to know if he made you forget me."

Suddenly Kate remembered to breathe. Then she remembered to open her eyes. She still didn't remember how to speak.

"Didn't think so," Justin said. He retrieved his bag of potato chips and disappeared back into the darkness.

TWENTY-THREE

It was without a doubt the biggest collection of muscles, tans, and big hair Chelsea had ever seen in one place—testimony to the powers of exercise, diet, peroxide, waxing, good DNA, and plastic surgery.

Mr. Scott was there, wearing a tiny bikini bathing suit that revealed as much as it concealed. Mrs. Scott was also there, looking like some Amazon goddess.

Chelsea sighed philosophically and waved her hand in front of Kate, who appeared a little glazed.

"These people are mutants," Kate said in a whisper. "I mean, look at that girl over there. Those boobs are bionic or something. No one has boobs like that."

"Actually, you're right," Chelsea said. "She

mentioned she'd had help from a plastic surgeon. Now, aren't you glad you decided to meet me down here?"

There was still more than an hour until the competition started, but Chelsea had asked all the contestants to assemble early in a meeting room just off the hotel lobby. Once she'd filled them in on all the details, she was supposed to lead the group out to the beach-front reviewing platform, where a crowd of spectators was already assembling.

"There he is," Chelsea said, pointing to a balding, middle-aged man wearing jeans and a HARD ROCK CAFÉ T-shirt. "That's Mr. McMurdo. My boss."

"Which one?"

"Which one?" Chelsea asked. "The one with the belly hanging out. It's not like finding Waldo. He's kind of obvious."

"Those two other guys behind him don't look like they're contestants either," Kate pointed out.

Chelsea followed Kate's gaze. Sure enough, two guys with neatly trimmed hair, blue windbreakers, and mirrored shades were moving toward Mr. McMurdo from either side.

"Hey, Chelsea, good turnout," Mr. McMurdo called out cheerfully. "Nice job. You really—" His compliment was cut short by the two men in windbreakers, who'd caught up with him and grabbed him by the arms. "Hey! What's the deal?"

"Edward McMurdo, you are under arrest at this time for fraud and for conspiracy to commit fraud. You have the right to remain silent—"

Chelsea's mouth dropped open. "Wait!" she cried. "You can't do that. He's my boss."

One of the policemen turned to give her a cool stare. "I'd advise you not to interfere, miss."

"I'd advise that too," Kate said, grabbing Chelsea's arm.

"But what's this about?" Chelsea asked. "I mean, we have a contest and I . . . I don't . . . I mean, can't this wait?"

As it began to dawn on the contestants that an arrest was taking place in their midst, a low rumble moved through the crowd.

"Look, folks," the first cop said, holding up his hands in a placating gesture, "I'm sorry, but this contest is off. Count yourselves lucky, all right? This gentleman is charged with rigging contests like this one and pocketing the entry fees without paying out the prizes."

"Untrue!" McMurdo shouted. "I run clean contests."

"Anything you say can and will be used . . ." the second cop said wearily.

269

They began dragging Mr. McMurdo away. "Hey, what about our money?" Mr. Scott demanded, stepping in front of the policemen.

The cop shrugged. "It's evidence right now. You'll have to come down to the station if you want to file a claim." He carefully maneuvered around the angry bodybuilder.

"You were part of this too, weren't you?" Mr. Scott accused, turning his fury on Chelsea.

"No." Chelsea gulped. There was something rather frightening about being yelled at by a big man wearing practically nothing. "I just worked for him for a couple of days."

"Yes, but you took our money," the girl with the surgically enhanced breasts pointed out. "If you did so with knowledge that you were participating in a fraud, that would make you an accessory to said fraud and every bit as culpable."

This was the girl who'd been bragging about her cup size? It was amazing how much smarter people could get when they thought they were being ripped off.

"I'm putting myself through law school with these contests," the girl went on, "and I don't spend three hours a day on a stair-stepper to be cheated. I have case books to buy."

"Look," the first cop said. "The kid's not involved. She was just a dupe. As for your entry fees, like I said, come down to the station." He paused to give the girl a long, slow look. "And if you'd like, miss, I can certainly give my full personal attention to processing your claim."

Mr. McMurdo and his police escort left the meeting room, followed by a growling spandex-clad mob.

"I can't believe this," Chelsea wailed. "He hasn't paid me yet!"

"Maybe you should go down to the police station too," Kate suggested.

"I'm not having much luck with jobs, am I?"

As the last of the contestants stormed out of the room, a woman in a brown business suit forced her way in against the tide. "I'm Sylvia Cohen, the manager of this hotel," she said to Chelsea. "What exactly is going on here? It looks like all the contestants are leaving."

"Yes, ma'am, they are," Chelsea confirmed. "See, Mr. McMurdo got arrested."

"Here? In my hotel?" Ms. Cohen asked, clearly horrified.

"Right here in this room, not five minutes ago. So I guess the contest is off."

Ms. Cohen's eyes went wide. "No. No, that's not possible."

"But Mr. McMurdo had all the prize money. Besides, all our contestants are on their way to the police station." Chelsea smiled to show she sympathized, but Ms. Cohen was obviously not in the mood for her pity.

"Listen, we built that platform out there, and we've been selling beer to a crowd of about three hundred people waiting to see this stupid show," she said. "Not to mention that it's the reason a lot of our guests chose this hotel. Besides, we've already taken money from the local beer distributor to hang his banners."

"There's obviously nothing my friend can do about that," Kate said reasonably. "I mean, she's probably never even going to get paid."

The manager froze, staring at Chelsea. Chelsea could almost hear the gears turning. Ms. Cohen snapped her fingers. "Yes there is!" She snatched Chelsea's arm in a painful grip. "We'll cover your wages and we'll put up the prize money. We'll get it back when we sue McMurdo for breach of contract. Only *you* have to go out and find some contestants."

"How am I supposed to do that?" Chelsea asked, trying to pry her arm free.

Mrs. Cohen waved her arm in the general direction of the beach. "There are thousands of airheads out there just waiting for the chance to strut their stuff. This will be their big chance. No entrance fee!"

Chelsea shook her head doubtfully. "I don't think—"

"Look, it's simple," Ms. Cohen interrupted. "One of two things is going to happen. Either you are going to refuse, in which case you'll be sued along with your scumbag boss. Or you're going to be a good girl and help me out in this crisis, in which case you not only get paid, I'll see to it that you get a decent job."

"That sounds like blackmail," Chelsea objected.

"It is blackmail," the manager agreed.

"Oh. Well, as long as we're clear on that."

"You have one hour." She spun on her heel and began chasing down an errant bellboy.

"Now what?" Chelsea asked.

"Well, I think I know where we can get some help, although I hate to give them the satisfaction," Kate said.

Grace stood on her tiptoes and tried to see over the heads of the crowd. Chelsea was working this event, and she wanted to be sure to say hi. Normally a Best Body on the Beach contest would be the last thing on earth she'd attend, but it seemed like an easy way to show some support for her roomie. Besides, there were tougher ways to spend a day than watching good-looking guys.

She shaded her hand and squinted, slowly scanning the crowd of faces.

"I don't suppose you're looking for me, are you?"

She almost chose to ignore the remark, but something about the voice was interesting. The face she found herself looking into belonged to an older man, maybe mid-twenties, with curly brown hair, a dark tan, and brown eyes.

"I don't even know you," Grace said coolly. "How could I be looking for you?"

He shrugged. "Haven't you ever found yourself looking for something without knowing it, and then finding it in the most unexpected place?"

Grace paused for a beat. "I have no idea what that's supposed to mean."

The guy looked a little sheepish, but undeterred. "Actually, I don't either. But it had that profound, deeply important sound, didn't it?"

Grace laughed despite herself. "You mean like *Today is the first day of the rest of your life?*"

"Or *When the going gets tough, the tough get going.*" He held out his hand, and after a moment's hesitation Grace shook it. She couldn't remember any guy ever coming on to her by shaking her hand. It was strangely formal.

"I'm David Jacobs. Nobody calls me Dave."

"I'm Grace Caywood." She paused, trying to remember why this guy seemed so familiar. "Hey. I know that name. You gave me your card, out by the airport. I was watching planes take off with my little brother, last Saturday, a week ago. I didn't recognize you without your motorcycle helmet."

He shook her hand, held it for a moment, then released it. "I didn't recognize you, either. Possibly because unlike the other day, you're wearing a bathing suit that should probably be illegal."

"I hope it won't distract you from the contest," Grace said.

"It may distract me from breathing," David said. "So, Grace Caywood. There are several follow-up lines that come to mind at a time like this. *Are you from around here? Do you come here often? You must be a model. Would you like to go for a drive in my Ferrari?* Any of those appeal to you?"

"Do you have a Ferrari?" Grace asked.

"Of course not. What kind of idiot would spend that much money on a car when for the same money he could buy himself a sweet little twin-engine jet?"

"So you have a—"

"Actually, no," David confessed. "I have a cramped little Cessna single-engine prop plane that starts to lose pieces when it goes over a hundred and twenty miles an hour."

"I've thought of learning to fly," Grace admitted. "I park out by the runway just to watch the planes take off and land."

Instantly she regretted her words. She didn't even know this guy, and already she was confiding in him.

But David didn't laugh. "I used to do that," he said, nodding. "Before I learned to fly."

"How did you learn?" Grace asked.

"If I tell you, you'll think I'm making it up," David said with a smile.

"Tell me anyway," Grace said. "I like a good story."

"I flew F-15's in the air force."

"Are those jets?"

"Are they jets?" David echoed in mock astonishment. "They're only the hottest fighters in the world."

"Is it true that's how you learned?"

"Absolutely."

"So how come you're not in the air force anymore?" she asked.

David's face went somber, shutting down the light in his eyes for a moment. Then he shrugged. "That's a long story, Grace. Someday maybe I'll tell it to you."

"Someday, huh?" Grace teased. "So in other words, to find out I'll have to see you again sometime?" She laughed. "Pretty sure of yourself, aren't you?"

"If I am not for myself, who will be?" David said.

"You know," Grace said with a grin, "that had that profound, deeply important sound."

TWENTY-FOUR

"Okay, this is now officially the stupidest thing I've ever done in my life," Kate muttered. She and Chelsea had been traipsing up and down the crowded beach for the last half hour, trying desperately to find guys to drag to the contest.

"Have I mentioned that I'm really glad we're not fighting anymore and that I'll owe you for the rest of my life for helping me get out of this jam?" Chelsea asked.

"Yes. Twice."

"How about that guy?" Chelsea pointed out a thin, curly-haired man standing at the edge of the water.

"Him? He's too hairy. I hate hairy guys," Kate said. "Don't you?"

Chelsea shrugged. "I'm open-minded on the subject. I mean, back hair I don't like."

"How about when it curls up out of their collar?"

"He's not wearing a collar."

"But if he were, he'd have collar hair, believe me."

"Fine. But we're running out of time, and so far you've vetoed every guy I've pointed out," Chelsea complained.

"You vetoed the guy I liked too," Kate said.

"He had no shoulders. You only liked him because he was reading a book."

"Not just any book," Kate corrected. "A *good* book."

"The man had spaghetti arms. I hate spaghetti arms."

"Oh, but collar hair is all right?"

"Hey, isn't that Grace over there?" Chelsea asked, pointing.

Kate squinted. "Over at the edge of the crowd? Yeah, I think it is her."

"Great. She's waiting for this contest to start just like everyone else, and so far we have exactly zero guys." Chelsea sighed. "This is not going to work."

"Do you think Justin and Alec and Connor did any better?"

"Sure, they're guys," Chelsea said. "They're used to walking up to girls they don't know and putting dubious propositions to them. You and I don't have a lot of experience going up to guys and saying, *Hey, dude, nice butt. Want to strut your stuff for me and a mob of howling, drooling women?*"

"You know, I think Grace is talking to that guy," Kate said, pulling down her sunglasses. "Maybe a friend of hers."

"So we're going to get Grace to do our dirty work for us?"

"She kind of does owe me a favor," Kate said hopefully.

"What do we got to lose?" Chelsea asked, throwing up her hands. "Certainly not our dignity. We gave that up long ago. I just hope this guy with Grace doesn't have spaghetti arms or collar hair."

They trudged across the hot sand toward Grace, who waved when she caught sight of them.

"Okay, now be a little subtle, all right?" Kate whispered to Chelsea.

"I've got ten minutes left," Chelsea said. "The time for subtle is over."

At least Grace's male companion didn't suffer from either of the deadly sins. As a matter of fact, he was a great-looking guy.

"Hi, Grace," Chelsea said, marching up. "Let

me make this quick—my boss got busted, the contestants all walked out, I'm trying to save my butt, and I need guys to compete for the guy half of the Best Body contest. Can I borrow yours?"

Chelsea and Kate burst into the hotel lobby, breathless, with a stunned and panicky-looking David in tow.

"There they are!" Chelsea cried. She pointed to Justin, Alec, and Connor, who were standing in the middle of a crowd of bikini-clad women.

"Of course," Kate said with a wry smile. "I told you they'd manage to round up a bunch of bimbos."

"Well, we have *one*, at least," Chelsea said, her voice edging toward desperation.

"Hey!" David protested.

"Sorry, David. I didn't mean you were a bimbo. In fact, no one's a bimbo. It's a stupid term. Everyone's a contestant."

"If Grace hadn't said she'd go out with me—" David began.

"Ladies," Alec called out, grinning ear to ear. "The Bod Squad has come through."

"Nine lovely contestants, all ready to have a go at fame and fortune," Connor added.

"Nine? I told you we needed only five," Chelsea said.

"Talk to Justin," Connor said. "He was quite the overachiever."

"He would be," Kate said, aiming a sour look at Justin.

"Ms. Lennox?" Ms. Cohen asked.

"We have nine girls ready to go," Chelsea told the manager. The woman nodded. "That's great. Where are the men?"

"Men?"

"Yes. You know—the contestants in one-piece suits?"

"Couldn't we just get by with female contestants?" Chelsea suggested.

"That would be blatantly sexist," Ms. Cohen pointed out. "Besides, there are a lot of women out there in that crowd, and in situations like this, the women are much more dangerous than the men. Trust me. I've been to Chippendales."

"I'm sorry, Ms. Cohen. I tried," Chelsea said. "Really. But we couldn't find any guys except David here."

"What's the matter with these three?" Ms. Cohen waved her arm toward Justin, Alec, and Connor.

Chelsea exchanged a look with Kate.

"Yeah," Kate said with a smirk. "What's the matter with these guys?"

"Not likely," Justin said, backing away.

282

"But these things are just good clean fun, Justin," Kate pointed out. "You said so yourself."

"Um, wait a minute, I, um—"

"And how about you, Connor?" Chelsea demanded. "You certainly don't object to copping a cheap peek, now, do you? Turnabout's fair play and all."

"Me? When did I—" He paused. "Oh. *That.*"

"I'm hungry, guys," Alec said suddenly. "Let's go catch a burger."

"Cowards." It was Grace, sauntering up behind them. "A bunch of wimps, that's what you are. I am so disappointed in all three of you. At least David here is prepared to help out when he's needed."

"I'm not going to do it," Connor said firmly.

"Don't you girls waste your time trying to manipulate us," Justin warned. "Hell will freeze over before I get up on a stage and flex my muscles for a bunch of screaming girls."

"Right on," Alec agreed.

"No way."

"We're outta here."

"I feel cheap and dirty," Connor grumbled as the six roommates arrived back at the house. "Granted, I often feel that way, but never more so than today."

"That's just because you didn't win," Alec crowed. "I feel fine myself."

"You shook your rear and pranced around, you cheating bastard," Connor accused, flopping into the worn Laz-E-Boy.

Alec cast him a pitying look. "The losers always have some excuse. I just gave the ladies what they wanted." He curled one arm and flexed his biceps. "Too bad for you they like a golden tan, rock-hard muscles, and, if I say so myself, a nice butt."

"Ladies?" Justin grumbled. "They were a mob. A mob with no taste."

"Yes, they treated you all just like so much meat on the hoof," Chelsea said happily. "Now you know what it's like."

"And you got plenty of applause, Justin," Kate said. She smiled at him innocently. "In fact, I was talking to your boss, Luis, and he said—"

Justin went pale. "Luis was there? Are you telling me Luis was there?"

Kate nodded. "I think he enjoyed it immensely. He kept saying something about how now he could make your life a living hell. He was actually giggling."

Justin sagged onto a couch, looking desolate. "He'll never let me live it down. I swear I'll be hearing about it months from now."

"Well, I cheered for all three of you, and David, too, of course," Grace said.

"I noticed he ducked out of there pretty quick," Alec pointed out.

"He had some business to deal with," Grace explained. "Plus, I think he was a little overcome. That girl grabbing at his bathing suit kind of made him nervous."

"That'll be the last you see of him," Chelsea said.

"I hope not," Grace said with a sly smile.

"I think the problem may have been my bathing suit," Connor said. "I don't think it showed me off to maximum advantage."

"Next time, try a burlap sack," Alec suggested.

"I think you're right, Connor," Chelsea said. "The cutoff look doesn't work for you."

Connor nodded. "I've always felt that concern about clothing was superficial and irrelevant. But then, I'm in America now, and a beach town to boot."

"Really," Chelsea agreed. "You're in the home office of superficiality and irrelevance."

"Maybe you'd like to help?" Connor asked. "I need to head over to O'Doul's to pick up my pay anyway. Afterward, perhaps you could help me in the small matter of buying a proper suit."

Kate stared at Connor in surprise. Unless

285

she'd just missed something, Connor was asking Chelsea to go out with him. Okay, not exactly on a date, but still—

"Sure," Chelsea said, putting on a casual tone that didn't fool Kate for a minute. "I'm always glad to help out the fashion-impaired."

The phone rang and Kate went to pick it up. "Hello? Lennox, Garrett, Caywood, Daniels, Riordan, and Quinn."

"You sound like a law firm." Andrew laughed.

"We haven't figured out how else to answer," Kate explained. "Use the street address? Just say hello?"

"Well, that may not be a problem much longer," Andrew said. "That condo I told you about? It *is* available. Right now. Two bedrooms, a slight bay view, quiet neighbors, and in your price range."

"You're kidding."

"No. But you have to take it by the end of today. He won't hold it any longer than that. I've been trying to call you for hours."

Kate pressed a hand over her ear, blocking out the sound of raucous laughter from Justin and Connor, and yells of indignant protest from Alec.

"I told him I was sure you wanted it," Andrew said. "So it's all set. No more housemates. No more hassles with old boyfriends. You and Chelsea can move right in."

"Um, that's great, Andrew. Thanks a lot. It sounds wonderful. But . . ."

"But what? I thought you were desperate to get out of there."

Kate gazed back at the living room. Chelsea had just brought in iced teas from the kitchen and placed them on the coffee table. When she sat down, Kate noticed she chose a seat closer to Connor.

Strange, she thought. *You think you know someone.* Getting interested in one of your housemates was probably a dumb move, of course. That was the problem with a coed household. Which was exactly what her parents would tell her if she decided to stay. They'd give her that more-in-sorrow-than-in-anger treatment, acting as if she'd lost her grip on reality. They'd tell her how much she'd disappointed them.

If she did move out, Chelsea would probably stay here. And she would miss having Chelsea around. The truth was, she'd miss having the rest of them around too. Even Grace. Even Justin.

Especially Justin.

Kate tried to imagine telling her parents the truth. It would make them more worried than

287

they already were. They might think that she had betrayed them somehow, deviating this way from a path they had all agreed on. They might worry that she had begun to change in ways they couldn't predict.

And she had. She'd begun to change in ways even she couldn't predict.

Maybe that was all right.

She sighed.

"That was a heavy sigh," Andrew remarked.

"I always sigh like that when I'm getting ready to do something stupid," Kate said. She told Andrew good-bye and sat back down on the couch next to Grace.

"Who was that?" Chelsea asked curiously.

Kate sighed again. "That was Andrew. He called to say he's got a great two-bedroom condo for me, and for you, if you want."

Chelsea looked away, frowning. Conversation stopped.

"What did you tell him?" Chelsea asked quietly.

Kate caught Justin's eye. What was that expression? Hopeful? And if so, hopeful for what? That she would leave—or that she would stay?

"I told him thanks," she said. "I told him moving there would probably be the smart thing, but I hadn't done anything smart since coming to

Ocean City, and I didn't see why I should start now."

"You're staying?" Chelsea cried. She ran over to give Kate a hard hug. "There's hope for you after all, Kate."

"Good decision," Connor said.

Justin nodded. "Great decision."

Kate looked over at him. He was giving her that wonderful, sexy, mysterious half-smile of his.

"So we are officially a house," Chelsea announced happily. "Roomies forever, or till the end of summer, whichever comes first. Well, that's a load off my mind. Now I can tell you about that phone call I got earlier."

"What phone call?" Kate asked suspiciously, as Chelsea retreated to a safe distance.

"Your mom. She called this morning while you were in the shower." Chelsea tried for an endearing grin. "Now, don't panic, we'll figure out a way to deal with it. They're coming next week for a visit. They're looking forward to meeting Justine, Alexandra, and your Irish roommate, Connie."

"Chelsea," Kate cried. "Why didn't you tell me this earlier?"

Chelsea shrugged. "You hadn't decided to stay yet. And you know how you are, Kate. You don't always do what you know you want to do."

TWENTY-FIVE

When Grace went to her room a little later, she was surprised to find Bo sprawled out on her bed, reading *Skateboarding* magazine. He glanced over the top of it as she came in.

"There you are," Grace said. "I was wondering where you'd gone. You should have come out. We were actually having a good time."

"Yeah, I overheard most of it," Bo said.

"Justin and Connor are forcing Alec to use his prize money to take us all out to dinner tonight. He specifically mentioned that you were welcome too."

"He's a friend of Justin's. I figured he'd be cool," Bo said.

"So you want to come?"

"I don't think so, Gracie. I . . . I kind of have plans."

"Plans, huh?" Grace asked. "Involving girls or skateboards?"

"Involving Mom."

Grace sat down at the edge of the bed, eyeing her brother doubtfully. "What do you mean, involving Mom?"

Bo set his magazine aside. "I guess I'm going to move back home."

"Bo, why?" she asked. "You know you can stay here with me."

He reached over and took her hand, a gesture that took Grace by surprise. "I know," Bo said. "And that's, like, the coolest thing. I mean, that you'd let me live with you and all. But—"

"What?"

Her little brother gritted his teeth, clearly fighting back a wave of emotion. Grace smiled wistfully. He was just fifteen and already trying so hard to act like an adult.

"Look, you have your friends here, Justin and Kate and all."

It surprised her to hear him call Kate her friend. Was she?

"The thing is, Mom doesn't have anyone," Bo went on.

"How about Darryl?" Grace asked sarcastically.

"She dumped him," Bo said. "I ran into her down on the boardwalk today. She said she blew

291

him off. And of course she promised to stop drinking and all."

"For the hundredth time," Grace pointed out.

"For the millionth time," Bo acknowledged. "I know it's probably a line. But she looked real sad. And the other night Justin was talking about how tough it had been for him without a father and all, and I started thinking, at least I can talk to Dad on the phone sometimes. I mean, who does Mom have, really?"

Grace put her arm around his shoulder and squeezed him tightly. "You don't have to go home to her just because she's lonely."

"Sure I do," Bo said softly. "Just like you have to take me in whenever it gets too rough, because you're my sister. Well, she's my mom."

Grace walked over to her window and stared at the water. The bay was calm and smooth, the way she wanted to feel. That was why she'd moved to this house, to smooth out the sharp angles and unexpected curves in her life. To simplify things. And yet, had anything gotten simpler since she'd moved here? She'd had to confront her old feelings for Justin, to face Kate, to stand up to her mother. And now she was faced with the gut-wrenching choice of whether or not to let her brother go back to the very place she'd run from.

She wished she had a drink. That would help her think calmly.

She turned away from the window. "You can't rescue her, Bo. She has to deal with her problems herself." She had to make certain he understood. It had taken her so long to figure it out for herself.

"I hear you."

"No matter what, it's her problem," Grace insisted. "It's not about you."

"I know, Gracie."

A tight knot in her chest seemed to burst, and suddenly, without really knowing why, she was crying. "I feel like I'm running away," she whispered.

Bo stood and draped his arm around her. She hadn't realized how tall he was getting. "You're not running away," Bo said. He let go, punched her shoulder, took a step back. "Besides, it's not like I don't know where to find you."

Grace impatiently brushed away her tears with the back of her hand. "Promise you'll come back? If things get bad?"

"Yeah. I promise." He gave her that sure-of-himself grin. "If you promise to stock up on munchies. Those cookies Kate buys really bite."

Grace laughed, then sniffled, then laughed again. "Look, come to dinner with us all first, okay? Then I'll drive you home. I need a date for dinner."

Bo gave her an incredulous look. "You're down to going out with your kid brother? That's pathetic, Gracie."

"You are my brother, Bo," Grace said softly. "But I think you've stopped being a kid."

"I suppose all this seems kind of tacky to you, doesn't it?" Chelsea asked as she and Connor strode along the boardwalk.

She'd been a little surprised when he'd asked her to come along. It wasn't as though there was anything going on between them. Still, she felt wonderfully comfortable and relaxed around Connor. Strange, when you thought about it, given their very different backgrounds.

"The boardwalk, tacky?" Connor pretended to be amazed at the suggestion. "Mile after mile of video arcades, T-shirt shops, caramel-corn stands, and tattoo parlors? Hordes of middle-aged couples in matching lime-green outfits, hairy fellows in black leather jackets, squalling children, packs of young girls smoking cigarettes and trying to look tough?" He looked at her and winked. "You call *that* tacky?"

Chelsea laughed. "I just figured Ireland was a little more classy. You know. Green fields. Charming pubs. Mossy stones."

"Yes, it is all of that," Connor agreed. "And the

sun shines about two days in a year."

"So, you came here for the sunshine?" Chelsea asked. She knew she was prying, but Connor didn't seem to mind.

"The sunshine is pleasant, no doubt about it," Connor said. "But I also came here because life in Ireland is much as you described it—green and charming and damp. I love it, don't mistake me, but it was getting a bit dull. Everyone there's an Irishman."

"That would make sense," Chelsea said.

"I mean, we all speak the same language, and have the same culture, and, for the most part, the same religion," Connor explained. "But here! In America, you have every race and religion and language. Every type, every variation. Right here on this boardwalk, I'll bet I could find you a Hindu or a Muslim. If you listen close, you'll hear Spanish and French and Japanese, and I wouldn't be surprised to hear the odd word of Bantu or Turkish."

Chelsea grinned. He was right. "Hey, in this crowd I wouldn't be surprised to hear Klingon."

"It's a fine place for a person hoping to be a writer," Connor said, surveying the boardwalk with a satisfied smile. "Never the same day twice. Always some surprise or other, waiting to jump up at you." He paused and pointed. "There's my own bit of tackiness on the boardwalk."

Chelsea saw the green neon, pale in the late-afternoon sky—O'Doul's O'Donuts.

"Great. I know we should hold off till dinner, but I could use a snack," Chelsea said. "It's been an emotionally trying day."

"Come on, then," Connor said.

Chelsea felt his arm slip through hers. It was a normal, everyday gesture, a casual, gentlemanly thing to do. So why did she feel something very close to a shiver skate up her spine when he'd touched her?

Suddenly a gaunt-looking young guy with a wispy mustache materialized out of the crowd and grabbed Connor's shoulder.

"Mick!" Connor said. "What are you doing out here? Old man O'Doul let you off early?"

"Are you looking for your pay then, Con?" Mick asked. His Irish accent was different and more pronounced than Connor's.

"Why else would I come by here on my day off?"

"You won't be wanting to go in there just now," Mick said in a low voice.

"And why's that?"

Mick jerked his head toward the doughnut shop. "Immigration. They're going over O'Doul's books right now. Me and Ian ducked out the back just in the nick."

Connor slipped his arm out of Chelsea's.

296

He gave her a worried glance. "You might be a little more discreet, Mick."

Mick looked over at Chelsea as if he hadn't noticed her before. "Oh, I see. Well, it's nothing, miss, nothing at all."

"See you, Mick. Thanks." Connor spun around and headed back up the boardwalk briskly. Chelsea had to hurry to catch up.

After a few minutes of walking in silence, Connor said, "I suppose you'd like some explanation of that back there, eh?" His voice was grim.

Immigration, Mick had said. It wasn't something that took a lot of imagination to figure out. Connor obviously wasn't interested in running into the men from immigration. He was in the United States illegally.

"Explanation?" Chelsea asked, struggling to control the wobble in her voice. She wasn't sure what to say.

"For what Mick said," Connor pressed.

Chelsea took a deep breath.

"Mick?" she said. "I didn't hear Mick say anything. In fact, I never met Mick."

Connor stopped and turned to her. For a while he just looked into her eyes. Then he took both her hands in his, raised them to his lips, and kissed them.

"Now," he said briskly. "About that bathing suit."

TWENTY-SIX

Dinner was wonderful. At Grace's insistence they didn't go to The Claw. She could never relax at work, she'd told Kate. Instead they went to a nice, quiet, seafood restaurant, where they spent a sizable chunk of Alec's winnings.

All during dinner they'd acted like housemates—chatting, teasing, laughing, almost like old friends. Even with the threat of a parental visit hanging over Kate's head, it made her glad she'd decided to stay in the house.

Afterward they wandered along the boardwalk, which was still going strong at eleven P.M. They started off in a group, heading toward the south end to the roller coasters and Ferris wheel, a mecca of bright neon. But after a while the group began to splinter. Alec ran into a girl who recognized him from the Best Body contest.

Chelsea and Connor drifted away on their own, still looking for a bathing suit.

Soon it was down to Grace, Bo, Kate, and Justin. The conversation had begun to grow more awkward, long silences interrupted by sudden spurts of pointless talk.

"I guess it's time for Bo and me to get going," Grace said at last, stopping. "We're heading back to my car."

"But we're almost to the rides," Kate said with just a touch of urgency in her voice. Part of her wasn't sure she was ready to face Justin alone. They had—what was it Chelsea had called it?—some unfinished business to take care of.

Of course, another part of her—the part she'd started to think of as the dangerous Kate—couldn't wait to get him alone. She was the Kate who'd done the unexpected things since getting to Ocean City. The one who'd moved into a household of crazy strangers. The one who'd spent her days getting cozy with sharks. The one who'd stood up to Grace's mother.

She put another step's distance between herself and Justin. "Are you sure you guys have to go?" she asked Grace. "Bo, don't you like roller coasters?"

Bo shook his head. "After you've done a fakie ollie into a backward front-truck grind down into a noseslide on the drawbridge *while* it's going up, you don't get too excited over the Mad Mouse, Kate."

Kate looked at Grace in bewilderment. "Translation?"

Grace shook her head. "It involves skateboards, but if I knew any more than that, it would just make me worry."

She sent Kate a sidelong glance, then leaned forward to plant a light kiss on Justin's cheek. "Good night, you two. Don't do anything I wouldn't do."

Bo winked at Kate. "Aren't you going to tell me how much you'll miss me?"

Kate laughed. "Come by any time, Bo. I'll stock up on cookies, just in case."

Grace put her arm around Bo's shoulder, and the two walked away.

"So," Justin said.

Kate nodded. "So."

"Want to ride the Mad Mouse?"

She shook her head. "I think I'll pass."

"How about a walk on the beach?"

Kate hesitated, glancing up and down the boardwalk.

"Chelsea won't rescue you," Justin chided, reading her mind. "I told her I wanted some time alone with you. Alec, too."

"Did you tell Grace?"

"No." Justin smiled. "I knew Grace would understand on her own."

He held out his hand. Tentatively, uncertainly, Kate took it. Together they stepped off the boardwalk onto the sand. In a few steps they were out of the glare of the boardwalk, almost invisible in the night. The warbling music from the rides faded and the sound of the waves took over, steady and soothing as a heartbeat.

They stood by the water, so close they were nearly touching. Kate surprised herself when she was the first to break the silence. "I swore to myself I'd never get involved with you again, Justin," she said.

"But you came back to Ocean City."

"You told me you were leaving."

"I told me my mom was moving away," Justin corrected. "I never said *I* was."

Kate took off her sandals. The sand was cool and damp. "I just assumed," she said at last.

"Yes, but you weren't sure, Kate, and still you came back." Justin turned toward her; his eyes were filled with questions. "I'd like to believe you hoped I'd still be here. I'd like to believe that if I'd been gone, you'd have been disappointed."

Was Justin right? Had she secretly harbored some hope that returning to Ocean City would

301

mean returning to him? She'd told herself Justin was only a part of her past. But had she believed it in her heart?

"If you hadn't been here, I would have been hoping to see you around every corner," she admitted. "Every time the phone rang, every time there was a knock at my door, I'd have hoped it was you, Justin. But—"

"How can you tell me all that and then add a *but*?" Justin asked.

"Look, it hurt when I lost you."

"No more than it hurt me."

"I can't take that kind of thing again," Kate said. "I promised myself I wouldn't, and then there you were again. And here I am again, on the same beach, looking at the same person, feeling the same feelings. I'll always be afraid of how it's going to end, and the only way I can make sure it never does end is to keep it from beginning."

"Too late, Kate. It started last summer."

"It *ended* last summer."

"Did it?" He caressed her cheek with his hand and drew her to him. His kiss was heartbreakingly tender.

She shook her head and spoke in a whisper, not trusting her voice. "Don't, Justin. Don't do that again."

"Why?" he challenged.

Suddenly, inexplicably, she thought of Grace, that day she'd come to see Kate on the pier. *It's the complications that make life interesting, Kate.*

"Why, Kate?" Justin pressed.

What? What could she say? That she didn't want him? That would be a lie. That the same problems and differences that had split them up once were still there, unresolved? That they were two very different people, with different goals and plans and ambitions and beliefs? That—

"Oh, to hell with it," she said. "I love you, Justin."

He smiled and pulled her nearer. "I love you, Kate."

"But it doesn't make any sense," she protested.

"It's not supposed to. It's love."

"Oh. Then I guess you'd better kiss me again."

"Yes, I guess I'd better."

TWENTY-SEVEN

Grace sat on her bed, leaning back against the headboard. The lamp was off. The only light in the room came from the streetlight outside her window, cut into thin slices by the half-closed venetian blinds.

She screwed the cap off the bottle of tequila and poured another glass, her second since dropping Bo back at their mother's condo. The first drink had drowned about half her guilty feelings. She hoped this one would drown the rest.

Grace could hear Chelsea climbing into bed in the room upstairs. She and Connor had come home half an hour ago, followed shortly after that by Alec. Kate and Justin had been the last to arrive.

Grace had heard them as they'd passed by her window, talking in low, intimate whispers.

She'd strained to listen as she nursed her tequila. Not that she really cared, of course. Just innocent curiosity. In any case, there hadn't been much to hear. A few minutes ago Kate had come inside—alone—and headed up the stairs to her room.

Grace finished the second shot of tequila and felt the glow in her veins. The muscles in her neck loosened and she smiled at the darkness around her. "So, it's straight off to bed for Kate," she murmured. "And straight to bed for Justin—solo."

A thought entered her mind, a wicked thought that made her laugh silently. But no, that wouldn't be very nice.

Grace sighed and let the idea melt away. Besides, there was something else she'd been meaning to do. She climbed off her bed, pulled on her satin robe over her matching nightshirt, and stealthily opened her door. The hallway and the living room were dark and quiet. She padded on bare feet to the telephone stand by the foot of the stairs. David's business card was in the drawer, just where she'd left it.

She dialed the number. It rang three times before she heard the recorded message. *Hi, this is David Jacobs. Please leave a message after the beep.*

Grace frowned. Well, it was awfully late for him to be answering his phone. She started to hang up, then thought better of it.

"This is Grace," she said. "I'm betting you remember me. I've thought it over and I want to learn how to fly." She gave her number and set down the receiver.

Grace crossed to the door, opened it, and stepped out into the cool, dangerous night. The moon painted the low ripples of the bay water with silver. High thin clouds scurried by, hiding the stars.

Soon, maybe, she'd be flying up there, far away, all alone, as silent, peaceful, and untouchable as any of those stars.

The wistful thought vanished in a fog of guilt. Bo was home again, she reminded herself. Living with their mother, living with a volcano that lay rumbling in wait until booze brought on another explosion.

Grace shook her head angrily. She could use another drink herself. The buzz from that last one had evaporated too quickly.

But it was a pity to have to drink alone.

Only drunks drank alone.

She climbed down the stairs and crossed the lawn, enjoying the yielding sharpness of the grass beneath her bare feet. The boathouse was quiet and dark. Still, Grace doubted that Justin was asleep just yet.

She knocked softly and heard Mooch whimper curiously. A moment later the door opened.

Justin's face was obscured in shadow, but there was no hiding the expression in his eyes.

Disappointment. She'd almost expected that. Of course he'd hoped it was Kate.

But beneath the disappointment there was something else. Something buried, denied, but still visible.

"Hi, Justin," she said.

"Grace," he said neutrally.

"Nice night," she remarked. "I was restless."

Justin didn't answer.

"I heard Kate come home. I'm a little surprised she's not here with you." Grace paused for effect. "You must be losing your touch."

Justin sighed. "That's not what it's about with Kate and me."

"Uh-huh."

"Is there something I can do for you, Gracie?" Justin asked sharply.

Grace reached out and trailed a finger along his chin. He didn't pull away. "Maybe there is, Justin," she replied coolly. She drew her finger across his lips, then pulled back.

"I'll let you know," she said. Then she slowly turned away, back into the darkness.

Don't miss the next exciting book in

O CEAN
C ITY

Love Shack

"Come on, Kate, do something," Chelsea Lennox urged, keeping her eye on the viewfinder of the video camera.

Kate Quinn glanced self-consciously at the nearby group of guys leering at her over sunglasses and noses thick with zinc oxide. It was early afternoon, and like most summer Sundays, the miles of Ocean City beaches were packed with sun worshipers. "Like what?"

"I don't know." Chelsea shrugged. "Don't just strike a pose. Do one of those supermodel moves, where you kind of leap through the air and smile at the same time."

"Is that what people usually do on the beach? Leap and smile?"

"Search me," Chelsea said. "I've only been a beach photographer for a couple hours, remember. My boss just told me the prices for still shots and videocassettes. She didn't tell me what people were supposed to do."

They walked a few steps over the hot sand, threading their way through beach blankets while ignoring the occasional whistle or proposition from guys. The air shimmered before them, a white-hot oven relieved only by the occasional halfhearted breath of wind off the ocean's surface. The sand burned Kate's feet around the edges of her sandals.

Chelsea struggled to adjust the two black straps around her neck. "These cameras are heavy," she complained. "If I keep this job all summer, I'll have the neck of a fullback."

Kate smiled. Somehow the high-tech photo equipment didn't quite go with Chelsea's outfit—a bright yellow baseball cap, an oversize T-shirt tied at her midriff, and a yellow bathing-suit bottom. Chelsea had painted the front of the shirt with a self-portrait made up of tiny dots of color.

"It's a definite improvement over your last couple of jobs," Kate said as she smoothly dodged a wayward Nerf ball. "You look like a real photographer."

"Uh-huh." Chelsea fiddled with a dial on the side of the camera. "I wonder what this thingy is, anyway? Come on, Kate, do something photogenic so I can practice. Give me a Cindy Crawford move—toss your hair a few times and pout."

"How about if we just forget it?" Kate suggested in a low voice. "I already feel like the whole beach is staring at us. And that's *without* any tossing or pouting."

"Oh, give me a break. You know you look great in a bathing suit."

A trio of nearby guys hooted encouragingly. Kate grabbed Chelsea's arm and pulled her toward the edge of the water. "That does it. You're going to have to stick to paying customers. I'm just here to read a good book and get a little tan," she said.

Chelsea eyed Kate's bathing suit and cocked an eyebrow. "In that new suit you'll get more than a *little* tan, Kate. You'll get just about everything tan."

Kate tugged at the strap of her glimmering royal-blue bikini. It was a recent addition, bought on a whim last week at a little boardwalk store called Full Disclosure. She already had two great Speedos, sleek, comfortable maillots that were perfect for the long swims she liked to take in the calmer waters of the bay. This suit, on the other hand, was perfect for standing very still and not making any sudden movements. "Is it too . . . you know?" Kate asked.

"Well, if what you were really doing is just lying out reading a book, it would be too . . . you know," Chelsea said, laughing. "But since I know what you're really going to do is lie out and read that book directly in front of Justin's chair, I don't think it's too . . . you know."

"Do you think Justin can see through me the way you can?" Kate asked.

"Sure. That's why you like him so much." Chelsea paused to train her still camera on a windsurfer skirting the shore, but just as she started to focus, the guy wiped out with a splash. "Not enough wind, I guess," she commented. "It's really still today." She let her camera fall to her side, where it swung lightly as she walked. "Do you think Connor can see through me the way you can?"

Kate grinned. "I don't suppose you're referring to the way you just happened to accidentally run into him in the upstairs hall yesterday?"

"That *was* an accident!" Chelsea protested.

"Uh-huh."

"There's nothing between Connor and me," Chelsea said firmly. She turned and gave Kate a sly grin. "Yet, anyway."

"Thought so."

"Besides, it'd never work, Kate," Chelsea continued. "I mean, he's Irish, I'm American. He's

311

white, I'm black. He's a pain in the butt, I'm—"
She grinned. "Okay, so we *do* have something in
common. Still, I'm not so sure about going out
with a guy I live with."

"I'm going out with Justin," Kate pointed out.

"Justin at least lives down in the boathouse.
Connor and I share a wall." Chelsea sighed and
looked away. She seemed to be about to say something, but then she stopped herself. "Well, I better
get to work," she said at last. "There's a beach full of
people wanting these magic memories preserved
for all time, or at least until their VCR eats the tape."
She took Kate's arm. "Come on. I'll walk on down
with you. That way it won't look quite so obvious
when you just happen to end up near his chair."

Justin's lifeguard chair was like all the others,
placed every block or so along the beach—a
whitewashed wood platform raised five feet off
the ground. He was sitting back, scanning the
beach, all the way left, then slowly all the way to
the right. His dark hair spilled over the band of a
white sun visor pulled low over his sunglasses.
His deeply tanned shoulders and strong arms
were visible above the rail of his perch.

Kate paused for a moment. Sometimes when
she saw Justin, a hot, dizzy, delicious feeling
washed through her, a realization of just how
lucky she was to have this second chance to be

with him. Last summer, they'd blown it. But this summer would make up for everything. This summer was going to be perfect, and what happened after August, when she went off to college and he sailed off into the sunset, well . . . she'd worry about that when the time came.

"Wipe that silly grin off your face," Chelsea instructed.

Kate laughed. She had a tendency to do that around Justin these days. "He does look great in those red lifeguard trunks, doesn't he?" she whispered.

"You're not the only one who thinks so," Chelsea pointed out, nodding at the heavy concentration of pretty girls lounging on beach towels in Justin's immediate vicinity.

"Oh, so you see them too. I thought I was just being paranoid," Kate said.

"Nope. But hey, that's life. Lifeguards attract girls. Good-looking lifeguards, especially."

Far out past the surf line, Kate noticed a beautiful sailboat, much larger than the boat Justin was laboring to restore. This was a real yacht. She looked over at Justin again. Not surprisingly, he was shooting glances at it between scans of the beach.

"Nice boat," Chelsea said.

Kate smiled to herself. Not a bad test. Could

Justin actually tear his eyes away from the boat and the beach to look at her?

"Hi, Justin," she called out.

Justin lowered his gaze, then lowered his sunglasses. He smiled as his gray eyes met hers, then traveled down the length of her body. His next smile had a different element added to the warmth.

He climbed down from the chair and took her in his arms, careful, even as he held her, to keep his face turned toward the water. "How am I supposed to concentrate on my work when you show up looking like this?" he asked.

"It seemed to me you were concentrating on that sailboat," Kate pointed out.

"What sailboat?" he said huskily, kissing her deeply.

"There, that's what I'm looking for—action." Chelsea focused the camera on Kate and Justin.

"Beautiful," Justin murmured as he pulled away, his eyes on the water.

"It is, isn't it?" Kate said, staring out at the boat.

"Actually, I meant you."

Kate smiled. She'd heard it before from other guys. But she'd always suspected they were just seeing the outside Kate, the tall, blue-eyed blond, the golden girl with the easy smile. When Justin said she was beautiful, she really *felt* beautiful.

Suddenly a concussive explosion rocked the air. Justin tore himself free of Kate's embrace and scanned the water, cursing under his breath.

Kate followed the direction of his gaze. The sailboat was an island of flames and smoke in the surrounding sea.

Justin gave three short blasts on his whistle. Then he snatched up a red plastic buoy and slung its rope over his shoulder.

"Justin!" Kate cried. "Justin!"

But he was already out of earshot, swimming like a torpedo toward a pillar of smoke that rose in deadly billows toward a cheerful sun.